# DISTANCE

# THERE IS

*Light*

# HARPER BLISS

## Also by Harper Bliss

No Strings Attached
The Road to You
Far from the World We Know
Seasons of Love
Release the Stars
Once in a Lifetime
At the Water's Edge
French Kissing Season Three
French Kissing Season Two
French Kissing Season One
High Rise (The Complete Collection)

Copyright © 2016 Harper Bliss
Cover picture © Depositphotos / a_lisa
Cover design by Caroline Manchoulas
Published by Ladylit Publishing – a division of Q.P.S. Projects Limited -
Hong Kong

ISBN-13 978-988-14910-1-5

*To my wife, who always dreams with me, no matter how wild or big.*

# CHAPTER ONE

●●●●●●●●●●●●●●●●●●●●

As they lower his casket into the ground, a part of me still believes this isn't real. That he'll push the lid off with those strong arms of his, pop out, and proclaim this was all just a really bad prank. I glance at the coffin as it settles into this grave dug especially for Ian, my Ian, and it suddenly seems to go so fast. Then, just like that, the casket is out of sight.

To my right, Jeremy can't hold back a loud sniffle. To my left, Dolores, Ian's mother, doesn't make a sound. I stand there, waiting for the punchline to this awful, strung-out joke.

"That's enough now, Ian," I want to say. "You've made your point. We're all more than ready for some relief."

Then Dolores' hand slips into mine, her fingers curl around mine in a desperate grip, and I stop believing in miracles. This is real. I'll never see Ian again. Dolores will never see her son again. During my thirty years on this planet, I've only been to the funerals of people I vaguely cared about. Distant aunts and relatives I never got to know. I'd always thought the first big one, the first one to tear me apart at least a little bit, would be my grandfather's. But I'm burying my boyfriend instead. Well, my partner, I guess. *Boyfriend* sounds so juvenile, so inadequate for what he was to me. When I told him, in jest, on my twenty-eighth birthday, that I was now of a respectable marrying age, he took me aside and, in all earnestness, proclaimed that he'd given the subject of marriage a lot of thought but that he couldn't do that to Dolores. She'd never had the chance to wed Angela, Ian's other mother, while Angela was still alive—the change

1

in legislation had come too late for them. Dolores, whose only child has just been lowered into a grave, and who is clutching at my hand with increasing desperation now—because who else is left for her to hold on to?—never struck me as the marrying kind. Perhaps that's because I've always only known her as a widow. Angela had already died before I met Ian. I've never seen her with anyone else.

"It's not so easy at her age," Ian used to say when I questioned him about this. "Especially when you've been with someone for such a long time."

Because I refuse to feel sorry for myself, I feel sorry for Dolores the most. First Angela, now Ian.

"She was ten years older than me and smoked like a chimney," Dolores once said, while heavily under the influence of a bottle of Merlot. "Growing old together was never really in the cards for us."

How different this is.

I give her hand a good hard squeeze back. Of all the people gathered here today, and there are many, I feel as though I can only compare grief with Dolores. Who else here—the artists Dolores knows, my extended family with whom I'm not close, my best friend Jeremy who lives every day like it's his last—can possibly know the depths of despair Ian's sudden death has caused? He was my soulmate. The sweetest boy I'd ever come across. The love of my life. And now he's gone.

Oh, shit. He's really gone. He's not going to miraculously rise from the dead. The punchline is the cruelest one ever, because there is none. I will never witness his smile again, will never hear him fake a British accent because when he was ten, he'd spent a summer in Oxford once with his dad, and he'll never again breeze into our apartment after work, always loud, always making sure I knew he was home, and joke, "What's for dinner, wife?"

I lost him. Dolores lost him. Our friends lost him. Even his ex has turned up for the funeral. We've all lost him.

The world is now without Ian Holloway. *My* world will never be the same again. And it's as though only now the shock, the woolen cocoon my feelings have been wrapped in since I got *that* phone call, is beginning to wear off, and the pain that's been lying in wait is starting to burrow a way through my flesh, quickly reaching my heart. In a panic, I look around. Ian. Where is he? The man who came into my life just at the right time. Who buffed up my self-esteem when it was at its lowest. The guy who, when I was about to spiral into one of my bouts of wallowing self-pity, would give me a sufficiently hard look and tell me to pull myself together— the only person who ever knew how to snap me out of that particular kind of funk. A person so seemingly uncomplicated, he managed to uncomplicate me along with him.

As I stand here, I curse myself for not pushing Ian harder to get married, because now I don't even have a ring, or a piece of paper that binds me to him after his death. I'm just a woman, a girl with no claims to make. I might as well be no one.

I turn to Dolores and collapse into her arms. I don't consider that she's probably not strong enough to catch me, and that my own parents are here, probably eager to put me back together, but not even on a day like this can I shake off the indifference that has crept into my heart when it comes to them. Dolores and Ian had become my family. As of now, it'll just be me and Dolores. She throws her arms around me, pats my hair with her hand, and breaks down with me.

# CHAPTER TWO

● ● ● ● ● ● ● ● ● ● ● ● ● ● ● ● ● ● ●

"Stop fussing," I say, wondering what I look like to Jeremy, who invited me to stay with him after Ian's accident. "I'll be fine." The funeral was four days ago and he has only left my side to sleep.

"Call me any time." He stands fumbling with his keys, shuffling his weight around. "I won't be home late."

"Go do your fabulous thing, darling," I say in the affected accent we sometimes use with each other, but it sounds wrong under the circumstances. Nothing has been carefree or frivolous since Ian died. Now there's before, and after. Because I'm still alive. When he left the apartment that morning, I had no idea I would never see him again. Often, I used to watch him scoot off on his bicycle—his pride and joy—through the kitchen window. When I craned my neck at the right angle, I could watch him until he turned the corner of the street. But that day, I didn't watch him. I was still in bed when he left. I barely kissed him goodbye, having pulled a late night the previous day trying to meet a deadline.

Jeremy sighs. "I don't have to go, Soph. I can take more time off. If anything, Amy Blatch will be exhilarated by my absence."

I'm not sure where I get the strength to get up and walk over to him, but I do. "You'll have to go out at some point. You can't always be here." *I'll need to learn to be alone sooner rather than later.* I put my hands on his shoulders the way he's done with me many times. "I'll be fine."

"Why don't you call Alex and ask her to come over?" He cocks his head, tries to look me in the eyes but his gaze slides away.

"Because Alex has her own life to live, and so do you."

A tear sprouts in the corner of Jeremy's eye. "Oh shit." He inhales deeply. "I'm so sorry. I can't stand that this happened. It's just so unfair." Words often repeated by now. Ian's death is unfair, unexpected, devastating. It's so many things that don't make him any less dead.

"Go." I really need him to leave. I don't want to fall apart in front of Jeremy again—it's all I've been doing the past week. "Bring me back some juicy gossip." My voice is breaking already. I all but push him out the door. "I'll be fine," I repeat, though, of course, I won't be.

Once Jeremy is gone, I take a deep breath. I listen for the faint ding of the elevator, wait for the doors to slide shut, then the tears come, again.

"Fuck," I scream. "Fuck, fuck, fuck."

Truth be told, I didn't want Jeremy to go tonight, but I also couldn't bear to ask him to stay with me another night. I could see how restless it was making him. Jeremy is the opposite of a homebody. We'd be watching television, both with a large glass of wine in our hands, and he'd be fidgeting, his foot shaking with impatience, his glance always darting away from whatever we were watching. I could have stayed with someone else, but Jeremy is my only single friend and I couldn't face staying with a couple, couldn't face the inevitable signs of intimacy, of a life shared and uninterrupted.

So here I stand, in Jeremy's starkly decorated apartment, alone. My eyes fall on a picture of Ian and me, a silly polaroid we took at Jeremy's fortieth birthday party a few years ago. Ian's cheeks are filled with air, like little balloons of flesh, his eyes bulging, and it makes me think of how hard it was to find a suitable picture for his obituary. Whenever a camera came near him, he would start goofing around. In the end, we used one I snapped of him when he was unaware of it. Ian staring into the distance, ruminating on something, his expression peaceful nonetheless.

"Get a grip," I whisper to myself. I hate this version of me, this beaten down, tearful, whiny woman I've become. Even though I know I'm *allowed* this devastation, this weakness—Alex called it vulnerability the other day—I can't identify with it. Every time I believe I've run out of tears, new ones show up, as though I haven't already been crying for a week. An endless supply of tears.

I head back to the couch and drink more of the wine Jeremy poured before he left—we've made a good dent in his stash. Then my cell phone beeps. Convinced it's Jeremy, texting me from a taxi, I sigh, but smile a little as well. Jeremy is exactly the kind of friend you need when something like this happens—something I can't wrap my head around, let alone accept. Because he's a bubble of a man, always ready to burst, to come up with an out-of-the-box plan, even though, of course, Ian dying has taken away some of his spontaneity and quick wit. The other day, I begged him to make me laugh, to tell me one of his outrageous stories I've heard so many times, but when he did, he couldn't put the right inflections in his voice to make it funny.

The message is not from Jeremy, but from my mother, asking how I'm holding up. Well-intentioned, I'm sure, but even now I can't read any words from my mother without hearing a persistent passive-aggressive ring to them. She probably thinks I haven't called her enough, haven't relied on her enough during these dire times. What am I even supposed to reply to that?

Knowing my mother, she's probably walking around the house, thinking of ways for this tragedy to bring us closer together. But some things are just beyond repair, like our relationship. I can't deal with this right now, although no matter how much my mother annoys me, at least it makes for a change from this relentless blackness that has wrapped itself around every thought I've had since Ian died. I don't reply.

I push my phone away and grab the remote control. Maybe Netflix will bring solace. As soon as I press the button, I know it won't, because how can it? How can televised drama possibly take my mind off the horror of real life? How can a sitcom ever make me smile again? Oh, fuck. I really shouldn't be alone. The loss weighs too heavy on me, the pain is too much for me to shoulder alone in Jeremy's living room. I reach for my phone again and call the person who reminds me of Ian the most, who knows him the best, whose loss is comparable to mine.

I call Dolores.

# CHAPTER THREE

● ● ● ● ● ● ● ● ● ● ● ● ● ● ● ● ● ● ● ● ●

"Come over," Dolores said. "Come right now." Her voice is still in my head when I'm already in the taxi. She's not his biological mother, yet she's all I have left of him. I'll never see the brown of his eyes in hers, never recognize that hand gesture with which he flopped his hair back. "You really shouldn't be alone right now." I could only agree. When I met Ian six years ago, he'd just put himself together again after losing his mother to lung cancer. Dolores has done this bereavement thing once before when she lost Angela. Not that I believe you can become better at losing loved ones.

Dolores' house is in the Gold Coast and I've always loved visiting there. It's where Ian grew up and his old bedroom is still reasonably intact. Even after Angela passed away, Dolores refused to vacate the four-bedroom property, even though it's way too big for just her.

"Oh, Sophie," she says when I arrive, and spreads her arms wide. Not having been raised in a very tactile family myself, it took me some time to get used to this family of huggers. Dolores was always throwing an arm around Ian, mussing his hair about, expressing her motherly love in one physical way or another. Now, she draws me into a tight embrace, and her arms wrap firmly around my neck. Instantly, my cheeks go wet with tears again. It's being here, in this house, where I always only visited with Ian, that does me in again. "I know nothing makes sense at all right now, honey," she whispers in my ear. "I know it feels like nothing ever will again."

When we break from the hug, I try to straighten my

spine, but it's as though my shoulders have been set into a permanent slump.

Dolores ushers me in, pours me brandy, and sits me down. "What was Jeremy thinking? Leaving you alone like that?"

"I wanted him to go out. We've been cooped up together for days now. It's not healthy. Besides, he had a work thing."

"Right. I'm sure I'll read all about it in this weekend's *Post*." Dolores says. "It will be such a delight." Dolores and Jeremy have a peculiar kind of relationship. She's fond of him, but she can't fathom his chosen profession of, in her words, "ridiculing Chicago's finest in his silly gossip column."

I ignore Dolores' comment and say, "I'm beginning to feel like a burden on everyone. It's been a week, and I'm only at the beginning of this while my friends are ready to pick up their lives again."

"You're always welcome here. You know that, don't you?" She looks at me over the rim of her wide-bellied glass. "And you're a burden to no one."

I nod. Dolores stares at me, as though she wants to say something else but doesn't quite know how. If this were Jeremy, or any of my other friends, looking at me like that, I would give them an annoyed "What?" but this is Ian's mother and there is a certain distance between us.

"After Angela died, I briefly saw someone. A therapist. She was good, even though talking to a stranger about my feelings isn't really my thing. I could give you her number, if you like," she says.

"It's not really my thing either," I'm quick to reply. Although I've never actually tried it.

"As long as you know the option is there," Dolores says. "That there are professionals who can help."

I try to picture Dolores pouring her heart out to a shrink. I don't see it; she's really not the type. Though she is not stingy with affection, she has a certain aura of untouchableness about her. It's not coldness, more a way of being on guard, perhaps because of what life has thrown at her already. I remember how intimidated I was by her when we first met. Ian hadn't helped by listing all his mother's accomplishments. He adored her, always claiming that he was still making up for being such a nuisance to both his mothers during puberty.

"From the day I turned thirteen until past my sixteenth birthday, I didn't want to be raised by two women," he said. "I wanted a man and a woman, or just a man or a woman, but decidedly *not* two women." Dolores has never talked to me about that period in Ian's life. I've only ever seen them be warm and loving toward each other—the exact opposite of how I am with my own parents.

I nod again, then drink from the brandy. My throat burns as I swallow, and I'm glad some sort of physical sensation is breaking through the numbness. I want to ask her so badly: *how did you cope when Angela died? That first week, what did you do? And afterward, that first year, and the rest of your life… where did you find the will to go on?* But these are words that won't make it past my lips. Not now, and possibly not ever.

I can't ask those questions of Dolores, whose life has been left in ruins just as much as mine. Besides, Ian told me how Dolores coped after Angela died following her long, draining illness. Dolores started another art gallery and became one of the biggest gallerists in Chicago in the process. She worked and worked, lost herself in the details of opening up a new venue, ignoring all the rest. Whereas I can't even begin to think about work. The pieces I write are long and inquisitive, requiring days of research—just me behind my laptop, in my office in the apartment Ian and I lived in.

An apartment Ian bought with his inheritance after Angela died. I don't even know what's going to happen to the home I once knew.

Dolores looks at me again, and I'm glad, because her glance takes my mind off the apartment problem, and off the prospect of having to find a new place to live, and adjusting to life on my own, with no one waking up beside me in the morning.

"Why don't you stay here tonight? There's plenty of room," she says.

I guess Dolores is not keen on being home alone either. I'd be doing her a favor by staying here, and perhaps this favor—however small—will make me feel something other than the crater of loss expanding in my chest. I nod. "Okay."

"Good," she says with the firm tone her voice gets when she agrees with something wholeheartedly. "More brandy? It will help you sleep."

This reminds me that I didn't bring my sleeping pills. Just in case Dolores doesn't have any, I hold out my glass to her.

* * *

As though the decision to stay at Dolores' house tricked my brain into relaxing—though I'm sure the brandy is more to blame than anything else—I sink into the couch, my limbs going loose. I let Dolores talk, nodding and humming when I think it's required. She doesn't ask me any questions, probably sensing that I don't feel much like engaging in conversation, that my brain is too blasted with grief to make an effort. I'm just relieved that I'm not sitting alone in Jeremy's apartment, waiting for an appropriate time to take a pill, go to bed, and lie in the dark for the most agonizing minutes of my day, until sleep takes away my consciousness. I really shouldn't go anywhere without my sleeping pills.

Sufficiently emboldened by the alcohol in my blood, when Dolores doesn't speak for a while, I ask, "Do you have Ambien?"

She quirks up her eyebrows, then shakes her head. "Have you been taking it for a full week?" There's no accusation in her voice, yet I feel put on the spot.

"Yes."

"Perfectly understandable, but you'll want to get off that as soon as possible. After Angela died, it took me forever to shake the habit. It's so easy to just pop a pill, until you forget how to go to sleep without them." She sighs. "I've hardly slept since Ian…" A pause. I know how hard it is to say the word. "But at least I know I'm not relying on pills."

"That's very noble of you, but I'm going to need something. Those couple of hours per night are all I have to not let myself be consumed by this. I need the respite."

"I get it, but you can't take a pill forever."

"I don't intend to, but anything is better than tossing and turning in bed, with no one beside me, realizing over and over again that I'll never—" My voice breaks. "—see him again."

"This is all I have." She holds up the half-empty bottle of brandy.

"Then I guess I'll go home." *Home?* What a joke. "I mean back to Jeremy's."

"It's late and you're exhausted. Why don't you stay and give it a try? You can sleep in my bedroom and watch TV. I'll take the guest room."

I remember the tiny favor I wanted to do for Dolores. We're in this together, after all. Just me and her. "Okay." Ian always refused to have a television in our bedroom, claiming it interfered with the quality of sleep. Now he's no longer here, I'm not so bothered with the quality as much as with the quantity of my sleep. "I'll let Jeremy know that I'm here."

# CHAPTER FOUR

●●●●●●●●●●●●●●●●●●●●●

I wake up with the television still blaring. I switch it off, afraid that I've kept Dolores awake in the room next door. Am I really in her bed? What was I thinking taking her up on her offer? Chasing her out of her own bed? The thought is so jarring that any remaining inclination toward sleep flees me. When I swallow, I have a bad taste in my mouth. From the back of my head, a painful pulse makes its way forward. Great, a brandy hangover in the middle of the night. I sit up, knowing I won't be able to sleep any time soon. As always when I wake after drinking too much, my heart hammers frantically, reminding me that, unlike Ian, I'm still alive.

I switch on the bedside lamp and cast my glance over Dolores' room. On the wall opposite the bed there's a picture of her and Angela in front of the Eiffel Tower. It was always just a fact of life that I would never meet Ian's biological mother, but now, for the first time, it hurts that I never shook Angela's hand and examined her face for similarities with her son. In the picture, Dolores has her arm wrapped around Angela's shoulder, clasping tightly, towering over her.

I met Ian's father for the first time the day before the funeral. A man with a voice so booming I searched for the amplifier he carried around with him. Robert, who insisted I call him Bob and certainly not Sir, is the only one left of the family he started with Angela thirty-five years ago. When he walked up to me, I believed I'd made a trip into the future and was clasping eyes on an older, surviving version of Ian —I believed that all the Ambien and Xanax I'd been taking was playing a trick on me. Bob was all Ian with his gangly limbs, easy smile and dark, full eyebrows. Seeing him, and the resemblance with Ian, only intensified my loss.

When he left Chicago a day after the funeral, I was relieved to see him go, but also sad. *There goes the very last of Ian,* I thought when I hugged him good-bye. *This is the last time I'll see those eyes and that hint of a smile that always played on his lips, even when he had no intention of smiling at all.*

I crash back into the pillows with a loud sigh. Dolores may have rules about sleeping pills, but I can't afford that luxury. Without a couple of hours of being out of it every night, I'd be even less of a person during the day. I'm of half a mind to just get up, get dressed and go back to Jeremy's. To swallow a pill and wait for it to deliver relief. But despite my mind being wide awake, my body doesn't have the energy.

I think of Dolores sleeping in the guest room, where Ian and I always stayed on the rare occasions that we spent the night. Perhaps that's why she offered her bed, a space not tainted with Ian's memory. Then my mind drifts to his former bedroom and I'm overcome with an urge to explore.

I tip-toe on the wooden floorboards, but can't avoid them creaking underneath my step as I head to Ian's room. When I turn the door handle, my pulse picks up speed, as though I'm expecting to find him there, as intact as his teenage belongings.

Of course, the room is empty.

I switch on the lamp on his desk, hoping it still works. It does, casting the room into an eerie sort of light. Before all of this happened, I would never have pegged myself for someone who speaks to deceased loved ones, but here, in Ian's room, I suddenly feel compelled to say something to him. To invoke his spirit. To, just one last time, feel the way I did when I was with him. Secure; more myself than I ever was before I met him; like I could do anything. I try to speak, but no words come out. Deflated, I head over to the bookshelf that is still lined with books. It's too dark to read the titles on the spines, but I let my finger slide over them, concluding that all objects in this room have recently been dusted.

I pick up a trophy and try to make out what it was for. When he first showed me his old bedroom, he would have certainly told me, but I don't remember.

Then I hear footsteps approaching.

"Can't sleep?" A whisper comes from behind me. I turn and see Dolores in the doorway.

"Did I wake you?"

"No," she says.

Through the darkness, I feel her glance land on the trophy I'm holding.

"Why did you keep this room as his?" Nighttime takes away some of my inhibitions.

Dolores shrugs. "He stayed here often when Angela was sick. After she died, I could never bring myself to make it into something else. Now I'm glad I didn't."

She looks different in the low light of the desk lamp, stripped of her daytime armor of fancy suits, meticulous hairdo and makeup. Dolores looks more vulnerable than I've ever seen her. More vulnerable than at the funeral, where she did cry, but not ostentatiously, and always held her chin up. Her eyes are red-rimmed enough for me to notice, in the feeble light, that she's been crying. At this time of night, there's no room for armor, and I see Dolores' pain to its full extent for the first time.

"I shouldn't have taken your bed," I mumble. "It's what you're familiar with."

"It's hardly the bed." Dolores makes a sniffling sound. She's crying again. All this falling apart we've done, our nerves raw and exposed, all this fragility, I'm so sick of it already, and it's only been a week.

At the funeral, my own mother howled louder than anyone else and I hated her for it. She was louder than me even, because I'd managed to wrap myself in a thick coat of stoicism, helped by a double dosage of Xanax.

"He was like a son to me," I heard her say to Dolores at the reception afterwards. I was too numb to be angry.

"What have you got there? Is that his wrestling trophy?" Dolores asks and takes a few steps toward me.

I give it to her; she examines it, surprising me with her eyesight though, of course, as his mother, she probably remembers what he won it for. She's just looking at the faded gold plate for show. Just going through the motions as we've been doing since we found out about his death. About the truck that didn't even touch him, but whose passage knocked him off balance enough to make him land headfirst on the curb, crack his skull, and die instantly.

"At least he didn't suffer," the police officer said, wanting to offer consolation.

"He only ever won one trophy. He wasn't that big on competition, but he was proud of it nonetheless." Dolores puts the trophy back. "We should go back to sleep."

I nod and wait for Dolores to exit the room. She doesn't. She just steadies herself, putting a hand against the bookcase. "Would you mind sharing my bed?" she asks, her voice so low and trembly, it instantly connects with that constant, throbbing ache in my gut—the knot that has kept me from eating a solid meal for days.

Again, I nod, as though her request is perfectly normal. In this moment, it is.

\* \* \*

Dolores and I watch television in bed until our eyes are so bleary, it becomes impossible for them to remain open. I must have dozed off for a minute, because the next time my eyes flutter open, she has switched off the television and the room is bathed in darkness.

"Night," I mumble and turn on my side, leaving the biggest possible gap the width of her bed allows between us.

"Night, Sophie," Dolores says, and the mere fact of

someone wishing me good night, simply saying a few words, is enough to make me sink into the mattress a little more deeply, a little more determined to actually sleep.

At first, I drift in and out, because the air is different in this room, and the light from the street lamps cuts through the sliver in between the curtains at an angle I'm not used to. But there's someone breathing next to me and it makes me feel like I'm not the only person left alive on this earth.

I listen to Dolores' soft inhales and exhales, to how the sheets shift when she does. And right before I nod off into real, deep sleep, before my mind starts tuning out and my subconscious takes over, Dolores shuffles closer and lightly drapes an arm over me.

# CHAPTER FIVE

● ● ● ● ● ● ● ● ● ● ● ● ● ● ● ● ● ● ●

When I first open my eyes, I don't know where I am. Then I realize I'm not alone. For the briefest of moments, I think it's Ian gently breathing in and out beside me, still lost to the delicious oblivion of sleep. It *was* all just a really bad dream. When I turn around, I see Dolores' face. Then it comes back to me. Her tears in Ian's old bedroom. Dolores showing me her softer side, as she stood there with her robe tightly wrapped around her, and then when she let it fall to the floor before she crawled into bed with me, baring the shorts and tank top I had never expected her to sleep in.

I remember the arm she gently laid on top of me, the comfort it offered and I grabbed with both hands. I remember that feeling of someone loving me enough to do that for me, to shove aside any possible awkwardness and just, out of sheer need, embrace me. *I am still loved,* was one of the last thoughts that flitted through my mind before I fell asleep, too exhausted to be astounded by my ability to do so unmedicated.

Dolores is lying on her back. While it's utterly strange to wake up next to her, the sensation of strangeness is washed out by the comfort of not being alone. I have to face the same dreadful realization every morning—every single time succumbing to a flicker of hope, just before waking, that none of this actually happened—that Ian is dead. That I will never see the love of my life again in the flesh. I try not to stir. I don't want to wake her. God knows how long she lay with her arm wrapped around me, waiting for me to doze off, unable to do so herself.

Her tears last night connected me to her in a way I haven't experienced before. In this dizzying, infuriating grief, we are equals. We are alike. We can understand each other the way no one else can. While grief is surely universal and people like Jeremy can easily empathize with my loss, they can never feel the true extent of it. And while I knew Ian in a different capacity than his mother, our love for him ran equally deep. I didn't just love Ian; I adored him. Not just because he was my partner, but because he saved me from myself, and from the person I would have become without him.

"Hey," Dolores' voice croaks.

That cold fist that has been clenched around my heart for the past week, loosens a tad at the sound of her voice. "Morning," I say, mustering a small smile, surprised that my lips can still curl upward.

"Did you manage to get some sleep?" she asks.

"I did. Thank you."

"No need to thank me." She stretches her arms above her head. "Have you been eating? I'll make us some breakfast." Dolores sits up and throws the covers off. She's not one for lounging in bed, then. Or perhaps she's no longer able to ignore the awkwardness of this situation. She doesn't even wait for my reply, but heads into the ensuite bathroom without another word.

* * *

"Have you gone home?" Dolores asks when she presents me with a plate of scrambled eggs.

The smell of food makes me hungry, but it's as though the loss has settled in my stomach and there's no room for anything else.

"No. Jeremy's gone by a few times to pick up some clean clothes and things I forgot, but I just—" I was at home when I first got a phone call from the police, asking me whether I was Ian Holloway's emergency contact, what my relationship was to him, and where I was. I was at home when the police rang the bell and I buzzed them in, seized by fear, because they'd asked me to stay put, and what else could that mean but the absolute worst?

It was at home that I crashed to my knees as they gave me the news, saying that he'd died instantly—that he hadn't suffered.

Our home where we lived together for five years, but which was, on paper, solely his. I paid him a token amount of rent, enough so that I could feel independent, but nowhere near the amount a place like his would usually rent for. Our home, where every single thing reminds me of him, and of how he'll never set foot in it again.

"Look, Sophie, I know your situation. I want you to know the place is yours. That's what he would have wanted. I'm sure of that." Dolores sits down opposite me at the kitchen table. The eggs on her plate don't seem piled nearly as high as mine. "The thought just hit me last night. On top of everything else, I wouldn't want you to feel homeless as well."

"I can't go back yet." *I'm not sure I ever will*, I add in my head, not wanting to insult Dolores' generosity—or perhaps it's just charity.

"We can go together when you're ready," Dolores offers, her eyes on me again the way they were last night.

I nod, thinking that it feels like ages ago that I walked into Dolores' house, although it was only late last night. Time has slowed, just for me, to make sure I feel every pinch of agony of Ian's death.

Dolores clears her throat. "Why don't you stay here for a bit? That way you're not cramping Jeremy's style and, truth be told, I could do with the company."

I glance at her, while I play with the eggs on my plate. The idea is appealing.

"There's plenty of room for both of us. I won't be here all the time. I plan to go back to work after the weekend. I need it. It helps me."

"I think I might like that." Maybe what I need is a mother, someone who'll take care of me like one, no questions asked.

"I'm glad." Dolores' voice is lower than before. "I'll be the first to admit I'm rather set in my ways after having lived alone for years, but I think we'll get along nicely." She offers a slow smile, and in it, I see all the reasons to stay. Comfort. Companionship. Shared grief. Homeliness. Jeremy offers some of that as well, but his companionship, I expect, will soon be coming with a sort of light relief I'm not ready to handle.

Jeremy has been my best friend ever since I started freelancing for *The Chicago Morning Post* seven years ago, and while he excels at conversation, wit, and flamboyant suits, he's lighter than air. He floats through life, from party to party, from man to man, as though there's no tomorrow. A quality I've always greatly admired him for, but which gets under my skin now.

Staying with Jeremy was the obvious choice. He's single, has the prettiest guest room I've ever come across, and a relentless sunny disposition. It never occurred to me to stay with Dolores, but now that she has asked me, and I've spent the night here, it makes perfect sense.

There's enough of Ian here for me to feel whatever is left of his presence, but not too much to make me succumb underneath the weight of it.

"Thank you." Out of gratitude for Dolores asking me, I shovel some eggs into my mouth. "I'll get my things from Jeremy's today."

"I'll drive you," she says, with that commanding tone she gets sometimes, and which Ian used to mock her for, straight to her face.

I easily agree. I want nothing more right now than for someone to make decisions for me, to make things as easy as possible, so I can focus on dealing with the really hard stuff.

# CHAPTER SIX

● ● ● ● ● ● ● ● ● ● ● ● ● ● ● ● ● ● ● ●

Jeremy's eyes grow to the size of saucers. "You slept in Dolores' bed?" he repeats.

I've met him for lunch, another pointless affair where I stab at food but don't swallow a whole lot of it. Instead, with a strange but welcome sort of amusement, I watch his ever-shifting facial expressions.

"You know I'm not one to judge, but it just sounds so odd," he says, recovering quickly.

"And you're invited to dinner at your earliest convenience." I look away from his gaze.

"Don't change the subject. You can't tell me you slept in Dolores' bed and then follow up with a dinner invitation. It sounds… like you've all of a sudden become a couple."

I chuckle. For the first time since Ian's death, a genuine laugh escapes me. Then I shake my head. "I know it sounds weird, but it felt strangely comforting to sleep in her bed. There was a tenderness between us that soothed me. It's hard to explain. It just felt good. And I'm currently not in a position to walk away from anything that will even remotely make me feel good."

"I agree, darling, I do. But you must admit you derived some glee from telling me you shared Dolores' bed. For which I'm very happy, by the way. Anytime you want to shock me for your sheer amusement, be my guest."

In the seven years I've known Jeremy, there aren't a lot of things I haven't told him. He's the only person who knows about that time I was so close to breaking up with Ian, I had already started looking through apartment listings.

He's the one who talked me out of it. Not because he's so skilled at relationships, but because he'd glimpsed the possibility of me, of the person I could grow into, with Ian.

"She asked me to stay with her."

"Of course she did," Jeremy says in that quick-as-lightning way of his.

"What's that supposed to mean?" My voice sounds more wounded than I'd like it to be.

"Nothing, Soph. I'm sorry. I was going to make a really tasteless joke. You know me, so witty I just can't stop myself."

"Save it for your podcast, will you?"

"Speaking of, now that you're staying with Dolores, can you ask her if she'll be a guest? I'm dying to interview her."

"Why don't you ask her yourself when you come to dinner?"

"I just might, but, well, not a lot of people scare me, but she does a little."

"It's because she doesn't like you very much." My turn to make a joke. It's the first time Jeremy and I have been able to engage in a bit of mild banter. I'm happy to find out that underneath the dullness that envelops my senses, I have some capacity left for humor.

"Dolores loves me and you know it. I've told you before there's a secret understanding between gay people—"

I hold up my hands to cut him off. "Spare me the speech, please. Just come to dinner."

"I know she doesn't wholly approve of what I do, but that's only because we are from different generations."

Jeremy's rise to fame took place in the early 2000s when he started an unscrupulous but wildly popular gossip blog, which he later sold, yielding him a small fortune at the age of thirty-five, a widely-read column in *The Chicago Post Magazine*, and, for the past three years, a twice-a-week podcast in which he grills Chicago's prominent about their personal lives and habits. The sponsorship he gets for one episode of his show is double what I make for a freelance piece of ten thousand words that I typically work on for almost a month—we did the math once.

"Yes, that's all it is." I smile at Jeremy, because I'm grateful to have him in my life. Grateful that he's so different from everyone else I know. I could never tell Alex or any of my other friends about sharing Dolores' bed, no matter how innocent.

"I'm just glad you're finding some sort of comfort," Jeremy says. I think he's about to reach for my hand and take it in his, but that would be too out of character. "By the way, Jackie O.'s been asking about you. She was very delicate about it, but, you know just as well as I do that freelance investigative journalism is a cutthroat business and it's important to remain in the good graces of certain people, like the editor-in-chief of Chicago's biggest newspaper."

Jacqueline O'Brien is the deciding factor on the biggest part of my income. I write almost exclusively for *The Post*, but worrying about money hasn't made it through the fog of grief I've been shrouded in.

When I just shrug, Jeremy says, "At least you have a sugar momma now."

Because only Jeremy would ever have the audacity to say something outrageous like that, I burst out in an uncontrollable fit of laughter which soon morphs into real tears of anguish and acute loneliness again.

"Fuck, Jeremy, I'm such a mess. What on earth am I going to do?"

"If you don't want to work, that's fine. But you should find something to occupy yourself with. Don't just sit around all day doing nothing. It will drive you mad."

"I, er, I've been thinking about something."

"Spill." Jeremy adopts only a slightly softer tone of voice than the inquisitive one he uses on his podcast.

"I've been thinking about… writing to him. To Ian." It sounds so crazy when I say it out loud. "I never even got to say goodbye. So much remains unsaid. It's not because I believe in life after death or anything like that, but just because it would make me feel connected to him again. I don't know. It sounds silly now."

"Soph, come on. It's not silly. If it helps you, it's great. Necessary, even. Do it."

I push away the plate of food I've barely touched. "Okay then, I will."

# CHAPTER SEVEN

●●●●●●●●●●●●●●●●●●●●

As we watch television in the living room, I work up the courage to ask her. Because all I can think of is her arm slipping on top of me again, soothing me, giving me that feeling of being loved again. I glance at Dolores while I scroll through the dozens of messages offering condolences on my phone, flipping through pictures of Ian and me, checking Facebook for distraction.

Dolores sits in the couch with a straight back, her shoes still on, as though she's visiting with someone instead of relaxing in her own home. I wonder if this is how she always sits or whether she's doing it on account of me being here.

We're watching *Grace & Frankie* on Netflix, a show Ian and I tried, but didn't think funny at all.

"If I have to watch one more minute of this, my eyes will actually roll out of my head, babe," Ian said, rolling his eyes in an exaggerated fashion, which was much funnier than any of the jokes on the show.

Dolores gives a mild chuckle once in a while. She seems especially fond of the Jane Fonda character, always shifting her position a little when she's on screen.

I was glad when, after dinner, Dolores offered to turn on the television. She's Ian's mother. She's family. But that doesn't make it so we can easily indulge in the silence that falls between us. Most of what I know about her is what Ian told me. Before Ian's death, I hardly ever did anything alone with her. I'm not the type to call up my boyfriend's mother and ask her to go for coffee. Besides, Dolores works all the time. If she's not at one of her galleries, she's looking for new artists to represent, networking with other gallerists, or attending some high-society reception. Until Ian's death, Dolores and I lived in vastly different worlds.

Once the credits start rolling, I grab my chance. I've learned to ask things of people now without much qualms. Life-altering grief will do that to you.

"I slept surprisingly well in your bed last night," I begin. "I think it might have been the proximity to another person."

Dolores looks away from the screen and rests her gaze on me. "My bed is big enough for both of us," she simply says. "We can watch another episode in it, if you like."

It's as though, in her glance, and in her words, I can already see the tenderness she will bestow upon me again later. This thing we have between us that succeeds in, however slightly, alleviating our grief. This new closeness. This wordless understanding of each others' needs and feelings. At least, that's how I feel about it, and I'm not going to disturb the fragile air between us by asking her how she feels about it.

Once we're in bed, me in the pajamas I brought over from Jeremy's—together with a bottle of Ambien stashed away in my toiletries bag in the bathroom, just in case—and Dolores in her tank top-shorts combo, which baffles me again, I think of how loudly Ian would have laughed at this. Me sharing a bed with his mother. He wouldn't have questioned it, nor have searched for any deeper meaning to it, but just mocked it endlessly.

"Some more *Grace & Frankie*?" Dolores asks.

I nod because I don't have the heart to tell her it's not a show I enjoy. It doesn't even matter what we watch, as long as there's noise to drown out the whimpering voice in my head.

Dolores doesn't press Play immediately, but runs her fingers over the space between us in the bed. "This was Ian's spot when he was little. He loved crawling into bed with us."

"Did you let him watch television in here?" I ask.

"I only got a TV in here after Angela died. To mask the silence, I guess." She takes a few seconds to swallow something in her throat. "Ian dragged it up the stairs for me, asking me whether I really wanted to go down that road. 'Once you get a TV in here, Mom,' he said, 'it'll be forever.' When he said things like that he reminded me of Angela so much. Physically, they didn't look much alike, but character-wise they were so similar."

I have to stop myself from grabbing her hand that's still stroking the sheet, and then I wonder why I would even bother stopping myself. I put my hand on hers and give it a gentle squeeze.

Dolores looks at our hands, but doesn't say anything, just inhales deeply—as though she's counting her breaths—then exhales. "I'd like to believe I shaped his character a little as well. He was only five when I moved in with Angela."

"Of course you did." I don't even need to think about this. I never knew Angela, but I've known Dolores for as long as I've known—*knew*—Ian. He introduced me to his mother barely two weeks after we met. "I saw so much of you in him, Dolores. He was such an endlessly kind, optimistic, sweet guy."

"He was a beautiful boy who turned into a gorgeous man." Her voice catches in her throat.

"Inside and out." I give her hand another squeeze.

"He could also be annoyingly stubborn and a pestering know-it-all, but let's not speak ill of the dead." Dolores' chuckle transforms into a little yelp. With her free hand, she brushes some tears from her cheeks. "Goodness, I think you'll have to hold *me* tonight." She looks at me.

"I will," I say, meaning it from the bottom of my heart.

# CHAPTER EIGHT

●●●●●●●●●●●●●●●●●●●●

*Ian, Babe,*

*It has been two weeks and two days since I received the awful, dreadful news. Since you left me for good. I don't cry all day, every day anymore, though the first few days, I truly believed I would never be able to stop. Because, do tell me, what the hell am I going to do without you? You were so much more than my boyfriend. You were my rock. My sounding board. The person who allowed me to become my true self.*

*Who will I be now? Without you, I'm not even sure I can be this person I worked so hard to become. I miss you every single second and your sudden, cruel absence is so big, so all-encompassing, there's no room for anything else. There's only this grief, bottomless and inevitable grief.*

*Most mornings, when I wake up, there's this split second when I'm convinced it didn't happen. You were not on Paterson Street when that truck started reversing. You didn't lose your balance. You were wearing a helmet. I mean, it's so unlike you to lose your balance like that. I just can't imagine it. You must have been daydreaming, must not have had your eyes on the road like a hawk, scanning for danger. What were you dreaming of?*

*And fuck, Ian, there have been numerous times, more than I'd like to admit, that I wished I were religious, so that I could find comfort in my faith, and believe that you are up there somewhere watching me, but sadly, I don't believe in any of these things. You're as gone as you'll ever be. I'm left behind. And, yes—and you won't like this—I have been feeling mightily sorry for myself. But you know what? I'm allowed. Because I have nothing left. Not even a wedding ring. Yes, you heard that right. I've also been wishing we had married. Then at least I'd be your widow, a scandalously young one, but at least something in relation to you. Now, I'm just a woman whose partner died in a road accident so stupid it wasn't even worth an article in a newspaper.*

*Well, fuck you, babe, for dying on me like that. How's that fair? I'm left sitting here crying, writing this stupid letter to you, which no one will ever read, in your mother's house. I've been staying with Dolores for a week now. It helps in a way to not be totally alone in this place of grief. We've managed to establish a certain coziness between us. She's such a nice woman, your mom.*

*Oh fuck, Ian. Fuck this letter. What's the point, anyway?*

*Sophie*

# CHAPTER NINE

●●●●●●●●●●●●●●●●●●●●

"Are you ready for this?" Dolores asks. We're sitting in her car outside the building where Ian and I used to live.

I huff out some air. "I'll never be ready, but I can't keep postponing it. I'll need to go back in at some point." It has been three weeks since Ian died. I've been living with Dolores for two of them. This morning, when we woke up together, she asked if I wanted to go home. At first, I thought she was kicking me out of her house, but she was merely inquiring about my state of mind and if it would allow me to go back to the apartment today, to grab some things, to sort through some mail, to stop putting it off.

We walk up to the second floor, climbing the staircase Ian used to maneuver his bicycle up. I suddenly wonder what happened to his bike. I never thought to ask and no one said anything. Maybe it's evidence, although Ian's death has been ruled an accident—as much his own fault as anyone else's. His death caused so little legal fanfare, it amplified the feeling that it didn't happen at all. Basically, he took a very unfortunate, nasty fall. A perfectly avoidable occurrence that happened nonetheless. As though someone somewhere pulled a string because his number happened to be up that day.

"Give me the key, sweetheart," Dolores says.

I've been trying to slide it into the lock for seconds, but my hands are trembling too much.

Dolores opens the door and we walk in. I don't break down as I might have expected, but that initial coldness wraps itself around my heart again. At the sight of our home, the place where we were so happy, I go back to being the woman who was just told that her partner has died. Three weeks don't make any difference, anyway. They might as well just have told me today. Everything is still the same. His iPad is still lying on the kitchen table. His shoes are by the door. Two of his jackets are hanging on a hook in the kitchen. Ian still lives here, even though he's no longer alive.

Dolores puts the mail she collected from the letterbox on the living room table. "You may want to sort through this," she says.

I glance at the pile. There's not that much. Jeremy has been coming by to collect the mail every other day and he stopped by Dolores' house a couple of days ago with what he had amassed. It's probably just bills, which will only remind me of how I should get back to work. But no subject can grab me to a degree that I'm willing to become passionate about it for a couple of weeks. Anything that needs investigating will need to be researched and written by someone else. Jackie O. will soon forget all about me, and I don't care.

My glance catches the large painting on the living room wall. It was Dolores' housewarming gift when Ian moved in, before I was his girlfriend. It's by a Japanese artist; an eye-catching piece in bright turquoise of a girl with a disproportionately large head and eyes. It's not creepy, just a little eerie, and anyone who ever visited this place could never stop staring at it. Ian loved that painting. He could go on and on about art, and he and Dolores often did.

I take a few steps and halt in front of our bedroom door. There's no way I'm going in there. Maybe next time. Maybe never. Instead, I go into the next room: my office. It has two desks side by side, of which one was supposed to be Ian's home office, but he always took his laptop into the living room. His desk is covered in remnants of my last project. A piece that I had just turned in about the industrial prison complex. It was the last time I spoke to Jacqueline.

She called me after I emailed it through and wondered if I would be interested in doing more lifestyle-related pieces for the magazine, like interviewing celebrities, and writing about the latest diet fads. I respectfully declined. In hindsight, writing something a bit more breezy would be easier now—and better for my bank balance.

Jeremy hasn't touched anything in my office. Everything is exactly the way I left it. The magnitude of everything hits me again when I realize that I've been missing my big computer monitor, that my eyes have been hurting because of having to adjust to a much smaller laptop screen—and because of all of the crying—even though all I've been doing is writing letters to Ian. Because this is my life I'm standing inside of. Our flat, where we built our life together. And I'm going to have to start making some decisions.

One decision has been made already. I'm not moving back here anytime soon. I can't imagine myself on the couch by myself, going to bed alone, eating dinner with only the television for company. I will stay with Dolores for a good while longer.

Even though Dolores said she would be going back to work, and has started going to the galleries again, she spends much more time at the house than I had believed she would. Moreover, I think she's doing it for me. Even if only to check up on me, and to make sure I have something for lunch apart from the delicious cappuccinos her coffee machine makes. Except for the little chats about Ian we've started to have just before going to sleep, when she allows herself to break down a little, I've been astounded by Dolores' strength. So much so, that I want to be around her as much as I can, so as to absorb some of it, or at least be near it and so I can perhaps, sometime in the future, follow her example.

I go back into the living room and, my legs feeble, sit in front of the stack of mail. There are two letters addressed to

Ian, because all the utilities are in his name. One from the gas company and one from our internet provider, whom we've asked repeatedly to no longer send paper bills, but keeps doing so. I'll need to sort that out. Let them know Ian Holloway will no longer be requiring their services.

The last letter in the pile is addressed to me. It's from an attorney's office so I immediately suspect it will be bad news. Quickly realizing no news can be worse than the one I received in this very place three weeks ago, I open the letter and start reading.

"Did you know Ian had a will?" I ask Dolores.

She comes to sit next to me and looks at the letter over my shoulder, then shakes her head.

"We invite you to set up an appointment at the office of Mr. Coates at your earliest convenience, to go over Mr. Ian Holloway's last will and testament."

"I had no idea; but Coates is the same attorney who handled Angela's affairs," she says.

"Will you come with me?" I ask without even thinking about it.

"Of course." Dolores puts a hand on my shoulder, as she has done so many times in the past few weeks, and her touch, no matter how brief or small, moves something inside of me.

# CHAPTER TEN

●●●●●●●●●●●●●●●●●●●

"Well, fuck me," I say as we leave Mr. Coates' office, forgetting for an instant that I'm swearing in front of Dolores.

"People *can* surprise you from the grave," she says.

I just found out that the money Angela left Ian when she died was much more than he needed to buy his apartment eight years ago. That more than two years ago—around the time when Ian and I first started discussing marriage and decided against it—he had a will drawn up leaving the apartment and the money to me. And that he had taken out a generous life insurance policy leaving the beneficiary, meaning me, a quarter of a million dollars if he were to die.

"I always knew he was a sensible guy, but I had no clue about this," I stammer, still trying to wrap my head around what I've just been told.

Dolores grabs me by the shoulders. "I'm glad he made that will, Sophie. I'm glad he took care of you."

"I don't know what to think." I shuffle my weight around in Dolores' half embrace.

"He should have told you. Things like this should not come as a surprise." Her hands fall away from my shoulders.

"He knew I would never have agreed to it. None of this belongs to me."

"It would have had you been married. And he may have believed I didn't know, but I knew exactly why Ian didn't want to get married. He could be really principled about some things. Some might even say stubborn. My best

39

guess is that it was his way of continuing to grieve for Angela. He was a massive supporter of same-sex marriage. He wanted it so badly for us, but we never got the chance." She puts her hands on my shoulders again. Money is all well and good, but it doesn't bring Ian back. "I'm not going to lie, Sophie. I've been worried about you," Dolores continues. "This means one less worry, okay? A big one."

I nod. "You know what we should do? Go to Cooley's, his favorite bar, and get drunk in his honor."

"Then that's what we shall do." Dolores has been such a good sport, she's been up for anything. Not that I've made many suggestions—this is my first. But she's been kind enough to take me in and take care of me without expecting anything in return.

* * *

"This was Ian's favorite bar?" Dolores quirks up her eyebrows.

We've just arrived at Cooley's. Sports bars like this are a dime a dozen in this city. There's nothing special about it, except that it's two blocks from our apartment and, more importantly, it's run by Ian's first college roommate. Tommy grew up in the rural Midwest, in some godforsaken little town, and owning a bar like this in the city was his lifelong dream. Ian made a point of coming here from the beginning, a year before we met, and grew so fond of it, he became one of the regulars.

"I always believed my son was a hipster who hung out in coffee bars with his architect friends." Dolores can't seem to get over it. This is a day of surprises for both of us then.

"Don't worry, he did that, too." We take a seat at the bar. It's the middle of the afternoon, and I feel out of place, but anything I feel these days that isn't that huge mass of despair bearing down on me is a welcome enough sensation.

"Did he bring you here?" Dolores has trouble finding a comfortable position on the stool.

"A couple of times, but I prefer hanging out with

Jeremy in uptown wine bars, where they charge you at least double for the same amount of alcohol."

Dolores narrows her eyes, examining the beers on tap. "I'm not having any of those." She cuts her glance to the bartender. "I'll have a double Maker's Mark, neat."

"The same," I say, though I'm not a bourbon drinker, but I'm betting on it being the sort of liquor that will numb the pain the most. "Is Tommy not in?" The bartender has no reason to recognize me.

"He's visiting his family. He should be back next week," the barkeep says, then starts fixing our drinks.

We wait for our bourbons in silence and I imagine Tommy, who came to the funeral, having to leave Chicago for a while because his good friend died so suddenly in an accident. Maybe that's what I should do. Skip town. Go on a road trip. Find myself again. Get away from everything that reminds me of him. Or go to Thailand on a meditation retreat and not speak for five days, only cry. But the fact of the matter is that I don't know what I'm going to do. An apartment in my name and a load of money in the bank don't change that. Either way, if I left, I'd miss Dolores too much. Her strong presence, her arm lightly slung over my torso before I go to sleep.

The other night, I woke and she still had her arm around me. She was fast asleep and I didn't want to wake her by moving, so I just lay there, trying to analyze what it is about her that calms me so much, that makes me feel that, possibly, this won't be the end of me too.

"Here you go, ladies." The bartender presents our drinks.

We pick up our glasses and Dolores raises hers toward me in a toast. "To Ian, for taking care of his lady. I'm so proud of him for doing that."

I clink my glass against Dolores' and while I'm grateful to Ian for sorting out his affairs, it also makes me feel inadequate. Like I'm someone who needs taking care of. By his mother for my emotional needs and by him, for my financial ones after his untimely death.

"I know it's a silly question, but what's wrong?" Dolores asks.

I take a sip of bourbon, which burns in my throat and all the way down to my stomach. "I'm well aware I'm a freelancer who hasn't been working, but that doesn't mean I can't take care of myself."

"I wasn't insinuating that, Sophie. Not at all. I merely meant that I'm glad Ian did right by you and that the money will make things a little easier for you during this difficult time. I've read your articles in *The Post*. I know how capable and intelligent you are."

Dolores' kind words make my eyes fill with tears. But I'm so sick of crying—and my eyes feel as though they really can't take another bout of waterworks—that I ignore the onset of tears, and continue. "I also don't want you to think I'm voluntarily taking something that belongs to you. You're his mother. You have rights, too."

"Angela wanted him to have an apartment and a nest egg. I think she envisioned the grandchild she would never meet using it for college." Dolores puts a hand on my knee. "I don't need my son's money. Imagine how crass it would be, how vulgar, for us to fight over Ian's inheritance." Dolores clicks her tongue. "But if it's any consolation, I know how you feel. I've been in your position. Angela was always the one with the money in our relationship. When we met, I had nothing, only my pride. I was fiercely independent, but there comes a point, when you become a family, at which you need to let that go. And you, Ian, and I, we're family."

I nod, thinking about what a class act Dolores is, how gracefully she moves through this world that can be so ugly and vile. "I've always regretted not having had the chance to meet Angela."

Dolores gives an unexpected chuckle. "She was quite

something. Irresistible is the best word that comes to mind. She was short but fiery, as though her words had to make up for what she lacked in height. That woman had quite the mouth on her." She goes quiet, stares into her drink. "Most of all, she was an amazing mother. She would have gone to hell and back for that boy. Even when times were difficult at home. When he was a sulky teenager and said the most hurtful things to us, she was always patient with him, she always listened, made sure he was being heard."

"He felt so bad about that. It was one of the first things he told me when we met. 'There was a time when I didn't treat my mother the way she deserved to be treated,' he said, 'and I'll never be able to take back the things I said to her.'"

"He was completely heart-broken when she died. She'd been sick for such a long time. She'd had two relapses. Whereas I could feel at least some relief for her, that she wouldn't be in constant pain anymore, Ian didn't see it that way. He always asked for more opinions, tried to find other doctors who treated cancer patients with experimental drugs. He couldn't let her go, which I understand, but, in the end, that's all she wanted. She was ready for it. As prepared as she could be. She'd had ample time to say all her goodbyes. This… thing with Ian is so different. So out of the blue. There's just no comfort to be found in any of it. It doesn't make the slightest bit of sense. He promised Angela that he would do great things. She asked me, just before she died, when it was just the two of us in the room, to take care of our boy, and now he's dead." A tear drops from Dolores' eyelash into her bourbon. "We need another round of these." She knocks back her drink and bangs the glass hard onto the counter, getting the bartender's attention and raising two fingers to him.

I finish my own by taking a few sips and, with every drop I swallow, the burning sensation in my throat lessens.

The bartender is quick with the drinks and just as he

plants the new round in front of us, my phone beeps in my bag. I've had it on silent on and off for weeks, the constant pinging driving me near-crazy, because every last one of the messages, no matter how nice in intention, is a reminder of the dreadful thing that has happened. I ignore it and reach for my drink.

"You're not going to see who that is?" Dolores asks.

I shrug. "It's just a message." The only message I want to get is one telling me there's been a terrible mix-up and Ian is somehow still alive.

"You never know. It could be important."

I purse my lips together and nod, staring at Dolores.

"It's true," she says. Maybe she nurses the same vain hope as I do.

"You're just like Ian. He was *always* on his phone, couldn't let a message or email go unanswered for a single minute."

"Nu-uh. That drove me crazy about him. We'd be having a conversation and his phone would light up and he'd be all over it in a split second. I scolded him for that, told him it was very rude to not give his mother his full attention when we were together. That's why it struck me that you're ignoring your phone. It's not of your generation to do so." She pulls her lips into a small smile.

"Now see what you made me do." I reach in my bag for my phone, playing along. "Don't you dare start complaining when I don't give you my full attention for the next five minutes."

Dolores laughs and the sound of it loosens something in my belly. It feels so good to have a silly little chuckle. Then I read the message on my phone and expel a deep sigh.

"What is it?" Dolores asks.

"Nothing. Just my mother." I put my phone away, unwilling to deal with my mother right now.

"*Just* your mother?" Dolores has already downed her second whiskey.

"Yes, just my mother," I repeat, then focus my attention on my drink.

"You don't have a good relationship with her?" she insists.

"That's one way of putting it."

"How would you put it?" she asks, while signaling the bartender for another round.

"I'm sorry, Dolores, but you're not someone I can discuss my mother with."

"Why not?"

"Because you're Ian's mother and, I don't know, I don't think you would get it. You and Ian had this great relationship, but children having amazing, supportive, understanding relationships with their parents isn't always a given. If anything, Ian was so lucky to have you and Angela for his parents. Let's just say I didn't have the same luck."

"I happen to be a firm believer in the fact that all parents screw up their children to a certain degree. Mine certainly did."

"I don't really want to talk about this. I don't have the energy for it."

She puts her hand on my arm. "Ian and I were very close, Sophie. He told me things. I know more than you might think."

I widen my eyes. "What did he tell you?"

The bartender brings over the next round. If we keep knocking them back like this, we'll be crawling out of this bar on hands and knees.

"When I asked if I was ever going to meet your parents, he told me it wasn't that simple. That you had a very complicated relationship with them and didn't see them very often. And that there was a big chance I might never get to meet them. Admittedly, it was a bit daunting to see them for the first time at Ian's funeral, though it's all a bit of a blur."

"I'm sorry for not introducing you sooner. I could always think of a very good reason not to."

"Why? They raised a beautiful daughter?"

I hold up my hand. "Please, Dolores, don't say it. I don't want to talk about it. I can't have that conversation right now. I really can't." I remember how, after a visit to Evanston where my parents live, once we were back in the car, Ian had been so appalled by my mother's self-involved behavior that he'd just said, "Fuck them, Soph. Just fuck them." And how liberating that had felt.

Who's going to say that to me now?

Dolores' hand is still on my arm and I don't want her to remove it.

She nods. "Okay. But please know that you can talk to me about anything you want."

"You are so kind, Dolores. So generous with your time and affection. I really appreciate that." After three whiskeys and touching on my mommy issues just a tad, Dolores appears to me as the perfect mother, the one I always wanted.

"My heart is broken too. I'm grateful to have you in my life right now." With that, she takes a big gulp of whiskey, makes a face while it goes down, and orders another.

# CHAPTER ELEVEN

●●●●●●●●●●●●●●●●●●●●

Although the entire drive to Evanston is depressing, as always, I can't help the nostalgia rushing over me. It harks back to a time before I knew better, when life was still filled with play and innocence. Back then, I easily shrugged off as normal my mother's minimal affection and maximum narcissism.

Today is Mother's Day and even though I could have easily cited my grief as a valid reason not to show up at my parents' house for the occasion, I didn't. Without Ian around to say "Fuck them", the guilt for ignoring them grew too big. Though I know very well this is just for show. We'll pretend to be a family that gets along for as long as we can, until the tension rises too high and I'll leave. I have the best excuse these days.

I bought my mom a bunch of flowers and when I give them to her she feels the need to give me a long hug—as though a hug from her will make it all better. All it does is make me cringe.

My brother and his wife are here as well with their two young children. Emma is five and Tilda three. The girls are shouting something at each other that I can't make out.

This visit, of course, everything is different, because Ian is dead, and my mother can't direct the spotlight solely unto herself. She has to compete with me for attention and sympathy, though my family's sympathy is the last thing I want.

On my way over here, I made one promise to myself and to Ian's ghost: that I would never give them the satisfaction of needing them. Dolores is my family now. And Jeremy. Alex and her husband Bart, and our other friends. My small circle in Chicago.

While I love my brother—we were always in this together after all—I feel estranged from him, too. Our lives are so different, even though we only live half an hour's drive from one another. But he lives in the same suburb as my parents, and it makes for a world of difference. I also never understood why he is so keen on having my parents so involved in Tilda and Emma's lives. He told me once that the shittiest parents often make the best grandparents, because it gives them a chance to redeem themselves for their past mistakes. I believe my response was, "Good for you, but too little too late for me."

My dad just sits there, mostly saying nothing, in his default mode.

"Tilda can already count to ten," Sandra, my brother's wife, says.

At the mention of her name, Tilda turns her attention away from her sister. She waddles over to the couch, holds on to her mother's knees, and starts counting on her fingers. Her big blue eyes shine brightly with innocence and being so alive, so young and unspoiled and at the beginning of everything. I suddenly realize that the last time I saw the girls was before Ian died. Do they even know their uncle is dead? If so, who told them and how?

Not having any nieces or nephews in his own family, Ian loved spending time with the kids. He was always making plans for them, saying that we'd go pick them up at their mom and dad's and drive them into the city, show them what life was really about—that there was so much more to it than the suburb where they lived. But then, as so many of life's big plans, they got pushed away by other things to do, by work, and the way life can just consume you, eat away time without you realizing it, until it's too late.

"High five," I say to Tilda and hold up my hand. She

totters over to me, always running more than walking, and slaps the palm of her tiny hand against mine. I look at her, at this child who doesn't know anything yet about the awful surprises life can spring on you, and I just want to hold her, press her against my chest, as if that will protect her for the rest of her days.

"Can your auntie have a hug, Tilda?" I ask her in a silly, high-pitched voice.

She looks at me as solemnly as a three-year-old can, her clear gaze piercing my heart, and throws her little arms around me. They must have told her something, because my youngest niece is usually not very generous with dispensing hugs. They must have instructed her to give auntie Sophie a hug whenever she asks for it. They must all have been talking about me for weeks. Now it all hangs unsaid in the air between us. I can almost see my dad straining to say something, but unable to find that magic string of words to break the ice with.

So we do what we've grown accustomed to. We use the children as a buffer—I'm just as guilty of this as anyone else. "What did you get your mommy for Mother's Day?" I ask Tilda.

This is Emma's cue to chime in. "I made her flowers," she shouts.

Tilda just mumbles something, but it's enough to rouse a chuckle from the room.

After the laughter has subsided, my mother says, "Thanks for coming. It means a lot." She's like a subdued version of herself today. At least she doesn't ask me how I'm holding up. I know that me being so absent from her life hurts her, makes her question her self-worth in a way she's not accustomed to, and though I'm sorry about the state of our non-relationship, this is the only way it can be. Because I've witnessed the change in myself. The more I removed myself from my family, the more confident and happy I became.

But now, *happy* is a word so obsolete, so ludicrous, so far-fetched that, for an instant, I think it doesn't matter anymore. At least I still have a mother to visit on Mother's Day. Then I think of Dolores, who is all alone today and no longer has a son to shower her with outrageous gifts. All I want to do is flee this scene and go be with her. After spending so much time with Dolores, a comfortable easiness has slipped in. We have a rhythm going that suits us both. When we have dinner, the silences are no longer awkward, but we find solace in them, because they are shared. Every night, I sleep in her bed, like it's the most normal way of sleeping in the world.

\* \* \*

After an hour of talking about nothing in particular and avoiding the subject of Ian's death, I've had enough. Though I haven't said much, and done even less, my energy has been depleted. I'm emotionally empty, but I already know that the drive back to Chicago, back to Dolores, will make me feel a little more alive again.

"I'd better go," I say.

"You can stay the night," Mom says, as she always does, even though I haven't slept in this house in more than a decade. It's just another one of those habits of hers that are hard to shake—and another opportunity for me to reject her and highlight the fact that I'm the sole reason for this distance between us.

I say my goodbyes, giving Emma and Tilda an extra-long hug, and take a deep breath before starting my car. On the way back to Chicago, I think of all the things that were left unsaid, about the unease in the air, only pierced when one of the kids said something funny, followed by an overly hilarious bout of laughter.

As I approach the city limit, I almost, out of habit, turn left to drive to where Ian and I used to live, but I quickly correct myself, banning every thought of the apartment from my mind, and head over to Dolores' house. My home now.

# CHAPTER TWELVE

●●●●●●●●●●●●●●●●●●●

Dolores is not home when I arrive at the house. She's left a Post-it on the counter saying she'll be back late and not to wait up. But I always wait up. I'd rather sit on the couch flicking through channels until after midnight than go to bed on my own. Going to bed together is what we do now. It's the pinnacle of the comfort rituals we have created. She goes into her bathroom, the ensuite to her bedroom, and I go into what I now consider as mine but is actually the guest bathroom. We go in fully clothed, and come out ready for bed. When I hop in next to her, the sense of relief that washes over me is indescribable.

It's not late yet and instead of plonking myself down in front of the TV, I go up to the make-shift office I've set up in the guest bedroom. It's just a desk with a monitor on it, my laptop and some chargers and pens and a notebook. Turns out that of all the things I acquired over the course of my life, these are the essentials. I don't need the fancy lamp I bought to cast its expensive light on me when I write. I don't need the colorful mug I drank coffee from every morning to start my day—one of Dolores' well-used ones will do. I don't need the noise-canceling headphones I used to wear while working, because up here, on Dolores' second floor it's always quiet.

I sit at the desk and start composing another letter to Ian. I write it by hand, which I'm not used to anymore, but that way no one but me can ever read it—because my handwriting has become terrible due to lack of use.

*Ian,*

*There's something I haven't told you yet. Something that will make you arch up those full eyebrows of yours the way you did when you made fun of something I said.*

*Dolores and I have been sleeping in the same bed.*

*I know it sounds ridiculous, especially written down on a piece of paper like this. I'm snickering as I read it myself. But you have to understand that sleeping in your mother's bed is the only thing that makes this loneliness bearable. Because together, Dolores and I are not alone. We have each other.*

*She is so strong, Ian. I can't believe it. Sometimes I think that having lost Angela all those years ago inoculated her against future loss. I'm not claiming she's not grieving for you, because she is, but the way she carries herself through this pain and grief is so admirable. I don't know where she gets the wherewithal to do it, but I'm hoping to find out. Because I need me some of that, babe. Any other person would succumb under the accumulation of loss, but not Dolores. Her spine is cast in iron. She doesn't allow her head to hang low. In that respect, she's also an inspiration.*

*Maybe I'm paying extra attention to it because today is Mother's Day—Dolores' first one without you, though she seemed unbothered by it at breakfast, but perhaps only for my sake—and I went to see my own mother. Which made me miss you extra hard. I have no one to talk to about this stuff now. You were the only one who got it, or at least the only one I could confide in and who wouldn't declare me mental. I know, I know, I'm doing it again. I'm feeling very sorry for myself, indeed.*

*I didn't tell my mother I'm staying at Dolores'. I don't tell her so many things and I figured she wouldn't like it, what with me never wanting to spend the night at theirs. The tension is just too much for me. Being in that house automatically strips away a layer of my defense and I get so instantly gloomy. It's like stepping into a time-machine and being transported back to when I was twelve and Tyler and I had just been introduced to yet another nanny.*

*Isn't it funny that even now, after your death, you're still my only means of therapy—*

"You're writing again." Dolores stands in the doorframe.

"Oh." I didn't hear her come home, nor climb the stairs.

"I didn't mean to startle you. I saw the light was on in here."

"It's okay. I was just… scribbling." I'm not telling Dolores I'm writing a letter to her dead son.

"That's good. That's something."

"You're home early." I turn my chair toward her.

Dolores leans her shoulder against the doorframe and nods. "I fled the dinner party. This woman I've never met, and who obviously didn't know about Ian, was telling us all about how her son had taken her on a hot air balloon ride for Mother's Day early this morning, to see the sunrise over Chicago, and I just had to get out of there. I just couldn't sit there and pretend that every single word of her story didn't cut me like a knife. You know how Ian liked to go completely overboard on Mother's Day, to 'un-un-commercialize' it, as he called it. The year after Angela died, he took me on a helicopter ride, because, as he said, 'I had to get a double dose of Mother's Day attention now.' When this woman was talking about her sunrise flight over Chicago, I couldn't stop thinking about that. Although I do hate that it's Mother's Day that is making me fall apart like this."

I get up, walk over to her and throw my arms around her. The entire action happens on instinct. I embrace Dolores and hold her tightly against me, and she breaks down on my shoulder. Loud, heaving sobs escape her and though it's perhaps ironic that I was just describing in my letter to Ian how strong Dolores has been, I don't perceive her breakdown as weakness. I know how hard it is for her to show all this emotion in front of me, to show her naked, true self to me. It's only because I've been staying here and we've built this fort around us, in her house, that she can do this. I'm honored to have her fall apart in my arms.

"Come on." Gently, I coax her to her bedroom. She sits on the edge of the bed for a few minutes with her head buried in her hands. I sit next to her and pull her close, put my hand in her hair, massage her scalp, the way she has done for me so many times.

When she lifts her head out of her hands, she wipes away some of her tears, and doesn't say she's sorry. And that's what I meant when I wrote that she was strong. Dolores doesn't needlessly apologize for her grief. It's in her; there will be a missing piece in her heart forever, but she's not afraid to own up to it. But to get to the other side of this pain, we have to go through it. There's no way around, over or under it. We need to let it consume us for as long as it takes to put ourselves together and start living with it, as a permanent part of us.

"Can I get you anything?" I whisper, my arm curved around her neck now.

"No." Dolores shakes her head. "Just sit here with me for a while longer."

And I do.

* * *

When we're both in bed, lying on our backs, with the TV off, Dolores asks, "How was your Mother's Day?"

When I just shrug, she pushes herself up on her elbows and gives me a look that does something funny to those knots in my stomach—I can't decipher whether they uncoil or grow tighter.

"You still don't want to talk about it?" Dolores asks.

"It's Mother's Day, Dolores." When I bought the flowers for my mother I wondered whether I should get a bouquet for Dolores as well, but I concluded it would be too weird. Now I regret not having given her something.

"So?" She shifts onto her side, supporting her head on an upturned palm. When she exhales, her breath tickles my cheek.

"It's hard to say things about my mother to someone who is also a mother. It seems so disrespectful."

"Like it's a you versus us-mothers situation? I'm not naive, Sophie. And I don't even know your mother, though she did send me a friend request on Facebook a couple of days ago."

"Please don't accept it." At the thought of the string of grief-stricken messages my mother has posted since Ian's death, trying to garner empty, social media sympathy, a cold shiver runs down my spine.

"I won't if you don't want me to." Dolores puts her free hand on my shoulder.

"I know it's not… conventional for you and my parents to not be better acquainted, but I've always wanted to keep Ian's family separate from mine."

"Good thing I'm not big on conventions then." Dolores smiles and pats my shoulder.

Her touch has a relaxing effect on me. "It's just so hard sometimes to dislike someone you're meant to love without question. Or maybe dislike is the wrong word." This is beginning to feel like a conversation Ian and I used to have. One of those talks where he just let me go on and on, get it all off my chest after festering for too long, and just listened patiently. His dark glance calmed me, his hand often on my shoulder the way Dolores' is now.

Dolores nods thoughtfully.

"My mother likes to pretend we have a close relationship, while I think we don't have that much of a relationship at all. She was never there. When Tyler and I were growing up, she *always* had something better to do than spend time with us. Her company always seemed so much more important than anything we ever did. Then, when she was fifty, she had this big moment of enlightenment, after she crashed from too much stress and work and not treating her body right. Her body shut down and we were meant to feel very sorry for her, and I did, a little, but it wasn't suddenly going to change our relationship. As far as I'm concerned, she's still the same woman who left the house before I woke up in the morning and came home long after I'd gone to bed at night. I barely know her. And now she acts all hurt about us not being close, while she was the one who was always absent."

"What did Ian say when you told him about this?" Dolores' question surprises me.

"I didn't so much tell him as take him to my parents' house a few times, after which he got the picture." I don't tell Dolores that it took me years to fully disclose the relationship with my parents to Ian because I didn't want to be the brat with two parents who whined to her boyfriend about them when he'd just lost his own mother. "Though, of course, the topic came up after every visit. Every birthday or anniversary party we were invited to, or rather, meant to attend. I always gave him the option to stay home. They're *my* family, after all. But he always came with me, which made it a lot easier for me."

Dolores' fingers dig a little deeper into my flesh. I'm interpreting it as her way of saying she understands too. "I've seen you change over the years. You've become so much more comfortable in your skin. You've blossomed."

I chuckle. "That's only because when Ian first introduced us you intimidated the hell out of me."

"Oh, please. Me? I'm a pussycat."

"You were very courteous, but also a little scary. A bit like a mother hen protecting her young."

"I *was* protective of him. His previous girlfriend, Mandy, ditched him so cold-heartedly weeks before Angela died. If I could help it, no one would have ever hurt him again. But life is not a fairy-tale. Ian learned that soon enough." Dolores shakes her head. "I couldn't believe it when Mandy showed up at the funeral. She wasn't there for Angela's funeral. I guess she didn't love him enough to go through that with him. She knew it was inevitable and she bolted. He tried to hide it, said things like 'good riddance', but I could easily tell her leaving had crushed him. Angela was dying, so he had a way of displacing his pain about Mandy. He didn't date for a long time after that happened. Then he met you. If I was in any way unpleasant to you when we met, you can blame Mandy. I was sizing you up, trying to gauge if you too would leave him when times got tough and break his heart."

"I know I hurt him sometimes. I think it's inevitable when you love someone."

"That's so true." Dolores lets her head fall onto the pillow. Her hand doesn't move. "But you made him happy, Sophie, and for that I will always be grateful. He died a happy, loved man, which makes it all much more unbearable in a way. Sometimes I can see it as a small comfort, you know? One second he was just happily pedaling away on his bike, on his way to a job he was passionate about, having kissed his girlfriend good-bye, and the next, he was gone. He wouldn't have had time to even consider it was the end, to take into account our grief, because in a split second, his consciousness went." Her thumb strokes my shoulder. "Am I being too morbid?"

I shake my head even though I haven't been able to see it that way. I just miss him. Every second of every minute of every day. I miss how we would talk like this in bed at night because in the morning there was no time for chats. Ian was always running late, always pushing the snooze button one more time.

"Do you want to watch some TV?" I ask, not sure if I want this conversation to continue.

"I'm exhausted," Dolores says.

"Me too." Fatigue suddenly washes over me. All the emotions of the day, heightened by my visit home and this conversation with Dolores, catch up with me.

"No more Ambien for you?" Dolores asks.

She must know she's my sleeping aid now. Her

presence, proximity, and touch knock me out better than any pill could.

"Nope. Good night, Dolores."

"Night." She switches off the light and this time, when darkness falls in the room, she doesn't just throw an arm over my upper body, but presses her entire body against the back of mine.

At first, it startles me, until I relax against her generous touch, and I let all the tension of the day drain from my muscles.

Within minutes, I fall asleep totally wrapped up in Dolores.

# CHAPTER THIRTEEN

●●●●●●●●●●●●●●●●●●●

"Still sleeping in the big old lesbo bed?" Jeremy asks.

Lips pursed, I nod, while remembering how, this morning, I woke up with the front of my body pressed against Dolores. I must have turned in the middle of the night and, in my sleep, searched for more comfort, my sleeping body believing I was throwing my arms around Ian.

"I agree that it's marginally better than sleeping pills, Sophie, but before you know it, it will be a thing you can no longer do without. You can't sleep in Dolores' bed forever."

"Is that advice or judgment?"

Jeremy cocks his head. "Have you ever known me to judge?"

"It's basically how you make a living." My reply is snippier than I want it to be.

"I may judge others, but never you, my dear, cranky friend."

"I'm sorry. I've been feeling so restless the past few days."

"Of course you have. You're bored, sweetie. You need to do something with all this time you have on your hands."

"You might be right, old wise man." I nod. "A lady of leisure, I am not." I must have written Ian twenty letters by now, all written by hand, then copied onto my computer, stored in a folder named *Letters to my dead boyfriend*.

"I know for a fact that Jackie O. is ready to be pitched to, Soph. She'll go for any subject. *The Post* needs you."

"I've gone over my notebook with possible topics many times, but I just haven't felt that spark. Any project I undertake is a big commitment and I'm not sure I have it in me."

"Then write something shorter, a subject that doesn't require weeks of research. It's just an idea, but you could interview me, for instance. Didn't they ask you to write more frivolous pieces?" Jeremy bats his lashes. "I'm as frivolous as they come, honey."

I burst out laughing. "That should definitely entertain me, though I wouldn't find out anything new, because I already know everything there is to know about you, down to all the sleazy details."

Jeremy waves me off. "Maybe you should ghostwrite my memoir. Or we could do it together. Your journalistic gravitas combined with my effortless wit and fascinating life. It would be a hit for sure." He waggles his eyebrows.

"There's frivolous and then there's so airy it's almost weightless," I joke. "It would barely take my mind off things."

"You have to know what you want, Soph." Jeremy scans my face with his gray eyes. Familiarity between us grew so instantly after we met that I never took the time to consider if he's handsome or not. He doesn't have the most symmetrical face and he always looks a little tired, but he's got bags of charisma and can charm the pants off anyone.

I plant my elbows on the table between us in despair. "I know. I'm a journalist and writing is what I do, but it would feel like going back to how I was before. As much as I want to work, I just can't face doing the same exact thing I did before he died. It doesn't feel right. I want to make a change. Do something different."

"If this is going to be one of those follow-my-dreams speeches, I have a suggestion for you." Jeremy leans over the table conspiratorially. "Maybe it's time to dust off that novel you've been working on for as long as I've known you."

I huff out a breath. "I haven't thought about that in years."

"Really? Because you sure talked my ear off about it when we'd just met."

"Back then I was just one of those beginning journalists with the same dream as every other journalist: write the next great American novel. I was just being a cliché."

"I'm just saying, Soph. You want a project and it needs to be something different, but something you're passionate enough about. Maybe now's your time to do this. You can afford to take time off. Why not lose yourself in an epic plot? I'll help you. I love making stuff up."

"It's not even such a bad idea." I look Jeremy straight in the eye.

He sits there with his palms facing upward, head slanted, as though wanting to say—without words—that he's always full of good ideas. "I wouldn't use what you showed me years ago though. I would start anew." I can always count on Jeremy to be straightforward.

I nod, my heart beating a little faster, my mind working quicker than it has in weeks.

"Now that we've sorted out some occupational therapy for you, I have another question. When will you be ready to attend social functions again? I was thinking about having a small gathering at my place. Nothing fancy, just the usual gang. Your friends want to see more of you, darling. We miss you."

"You see me all the time," I say evasively, knowing it's hardly true.

"Correction: I *used* to see you all the time. Now I'm lucky if I get to see my best buddy once a week. That's not how we are. We are closer than that."

"I know." It's just been so cozy at Dolores' house. Whenever I refused an invitation, always carefully crafted and with plenty of options built-in to give me an easy way out, my first thought was always that it would make me miss Dolores too much. Just having her around, staying at her house, my ears perking up when I hear her come home. Maybe Jeremy is right. I'm leaning on Dolores too much. It has been almost two months. I can't hibernate with my mother-in-law forever. "I'll come to your party."

"Oh, it's not a party at all. Just a bunch of friends hanging out together. You and me. Alex and Bart. Sydney and Ethan. Bo and Cindy, if you want them there. And maybe Brandon… You have complete veto right over the guest list."

"That sounds fine, Jeremy. Thank you."

"No need to thank me yet. How about this Saturday? We'll start early. You can stay the night."

With a new kind of determination simmering inside of me, I agree.

"Oh, and one of our friends won't be drinking, if you know what I mean." He gives me an exaggerated wink.

"I don't. What *do* you mean?"

"One of them is up the duff, with child, has a bun in the oven."

"Really? Who?"

Jeremy folds his features into that irresistible apologetic pout he does so well. "I'm not supposed to say. But see what I mean, Soph? You've missed all the gossip."

"Is it Alex?" She and Bart have been trying for a while.

"My lips are sealed, but you'll find out on Saturday." While he says this, Jeremy gives a slight downward jerk with his chin. It's barely a nod, but it says enough.

Alex is one of my best friends and she hasn't been able to tell me her good news. It really is time to come out of hiding.

# CHAPTER FOURTEEN

● ● ● ● ● ● ● ● ● ● ● ● ● ● ● ● ● ● ● ●

"Come here," Dolores says, and throws her arms wide.

I step into her embrace and whereas before I'd have just let her hug me, now I hug back firmly, all my intention behind it.

She kisses me on the top of my head, and says, "I'm proud of you for doing this."

By the way we're standing in the hallway so dramatically, you'd think I'm leaving on a month-long expedition to the North Pole, while I'm only just going to Jeremy's house for a party and a sleepover.

We don't say it out loud, but it hangs in the air between us. We'll both be sleeping alone tonight. I've taken naps on my own. I've stayed in bed in the morning on my own after Dolores has gotten up to go to work. But never, in the past two months, have I gone to bed without her.

"I'll see you tomorrow." I step out of our embrace, which was lingering and a little unsettling because it makes me wonder whether Dolores will be all right on her own.

"Have fun," she says. I swear there's an undertone of sadness in her voice, more than usual, or perhaps it's just my imagination.

On the way over to Jeremy's, I clasp my hands around the steering wheel so tightly my knuckles are white by the time I arrive. I take a couple of deep breaths, reminding myself that these people are my friends. They've known me for years. But, despite having been to Jeremy's many times since Ian died, walking into his apartment now feels like stepping into a different world entirely.

* * *

After I've been hugged extensively and much longer than I would have been *before*, Alex pulls me aside, into the kitchen, where she shoos Jeremy out, and says, "Oh, Soph, I've missed you so much."

I'm glad that Jeremy already spilled the beans about her pregnancy, so I had time to adjust to the idea that for everyone else life goes on. New life is being created. Couples take the next steps that Ian and I will never take. Though he's not the king of discretion, I suspect that's the exact reason Jeremy didn't keep his mouth shut as he was most likely instructed to do.

We go through the motions of her asking me how I've been doing and me inquiring about her life. Then she says, "I didn't know when to tell you, but Bart and I are expecting. We're going to have a baby."

I give her a big smile—I don't have it in me to clasp my hands in front of my mouth in fake surprise. "That's really wonderful. I'm so happy for you." I pull her into a hug and when I stand with my arms around my friend, a person whom I wish nothing but well in this world, a pang of jealousy lances through me. Because for her, nothing much has changed, while for me, everything is still as broken as it was two months ago. Even my coming to this *gathering*, which is really a party—but couldn't possibly be called that —doesn't alter this situation.

"I shall raise a glass to your good news, Alex."

"I was a bit nervous about telling you," she says. "But I've got quite a belly on me now." She points at her stomach, which protrudes ever so slightly. If you didn't know, you wouldn't be able to tell just by looking at her.

I smile widely and try to gather myself, pull myself together and push back the anger that's boiling up within me. It's not as if Ian and I had decided that we wanted to have children. But now we don't even have the option anymore. Maybe I should check with that attorney, Mr.

Coates. Considering Ian was so practical about what would happen after his death, perhaps he had some of his sperm frozen without telling me.

I realize this sudden burst of anger isn't aimed at Alex; it's directed at Ian, for leaving me like that. For not being more careful. For not staying the hell alive. It's not that hard. Look at all the people at this party. They're all alive. Why them and not him? Why did he have to be the one to die?

"Are you okay?" Alex asks, her hands on the exact same spot on my upper arms where so many people have planted their sweaty palms since Ian's death. It's not on my shoulders, but just below. The imprints I have amassed there, as though the press of a palm in that exact spot can inject me with a secret force, a newfound inner strength stemming from the energy of the palm-planting party, and make it all okay.

I know I'm being unfair, and that everybody is just doing the best they can under the circumstances. But so am I. This angry person who feels so unfairly treated by life is the best version of myself I can be at this moment.

I need a drink.

"Yes," I say, resolutely, my mind on nothing but pouring some of the Veuve Clicquot Jeremy always treats us to at one of his parties down my throat. Tonight, I want to forget. I want to listen to my friends talk about their lives, moan about their jobs, argue about politics, gossip about colleagues, as though Ian were still alive but simply couldn't make it to the party. He's at home with a migraine and he didn't want me to stay with him; it would only make him feel worse. He forced me to come here and have a good time with my friends.

I can't pour the champagne down my throat fast enough to keep the fantasy alive.

* * *

"Hey there, Miss Thirsty," Jeremy says while he replenishes my glass. "You're going to regret this so much in the morning, but I'm not going to be the one to keep you from drinking your tits off tonight. Oh no, not me." He grins, then kisses me on the cheek.

I glance at the kitchen wall where he has lined up all the bottles we've emptied tonight, and I might be seeing double, but there are at least ten already. Apart from Alex, my friends are all drinking with me. We're doing this together. Getting mindlessly, recklessly wasted together, because what else are we going to do? The more we collectively drink, the more stories about Ian come to the surface.

His best friend Ethan, whom I've always found a little weird with his hippy man-bun and very socialist ideas, says, "The thing about Ian was that he was willing to believe everything anyone told him. He always gave you the benefit of the doubt, no matter how crazy the idea you put to him." For a socialist, he's enjoying the Veuve with a lot of gusto, knocking back the last of his glass in a fluid backward motion of his head. Then he continues. "Let's drink to Ian." His voice cracks and he grabs his wife Sydney's shoulder. He raises his glass nonetheless, even though it's empty. A guy Brandon brought to the party presents the bottle for a refill, because Jeremy seems to have grown tired of topping up drinks.

Ethan locks his gaze on me, gives a small nod of the head, and a tear glistens in the corner of his eye. Through the haze of alcohol, I realize that so many people have been missing him like crazy. That I'm not as alone as I thought I was, during those first weeks of grieving, when the pain was too great to think of anything or anyone else. Our friends' lives have been crushed, too.

No matter how drunk I am, I have enough presence of mind to realize that being here with my friends is good for me. These people whom we had built our lives with and around. Ethan and Bart, whom Ian went on fishing weekends with, never bringing back anything resembling fish. Jeremy, whom Ian had long discussions with about

LGBT rights and about how, even though same-sex marriage was now a fact, the battle was a long way from over. And Bo and Cindy, always referred to by everyone as "The Girls", who were friends of Jeremy's first, but whom Ian was always trying to meet up with and getting to know better because he admired them so much as a couple—and, perhaps, because they reminded him of Angela and Dolores when they were younger.

The love we share for him is magnified by us being here together, remembering him, toasting him, having a good old party in his honor, which he would have vastly preferred we do rather than mope about and succumb to infinite sadness. That's why I allow myself to give in to the vibe of this night, to let the atmosphere, and the copious amounts of alcohol, carry me through, no matter the consequences tomorrow. A hangover is really the last of my worries.

After taxis have been summoned and everyone has left, and I make a feeble attempt at helping Jeremy clean up a little of the mess, he says, "I will have none of that, princess." He swats a napkin from my hand. "Sit down and relax. Drink some water while you're at it."

"Is now an appropriate time to thank you?" I ask.

He sits next to me. "The best way to thank me is to get out more. This was good, wasn't it? It did you good."

I nod.

"You must be tired. All that hugging and crying and drinking. It tends to wear a person out."

"I'm exhausted."

"Why don't you go to bed?" He puts a hand on the small of my back. "Come on, I'll tuck you in."

With a loud sigh, I push myself off the couch. The heartwarming nature of tonight's party has thawed the ice around my soul a little, but now I have to go to bed alone. In my fantasy, in which Ian is still alive, just in bed with a migraine, I'd go home to a warm bed, fling my arms around him and cozy up to his strong body. Walking to Jeremy's guest bedroom, where I stayed when I was at my worst, puts an abrupt end to that foolish piece of make-believe.

I stand in the doorway, Jeremy behind me, and I look at the empty bed. I stare at it for what feels like forever and don't move, because I know I can't do it. I can't slip underneath its covers and fall asleep, not even with the amount of alcohol I've had and which is nearly knocking me to my knees. I simply can't. An invisible barrier has been thrown up between me and the bed.

I need Dolores.

"What is it?" Jeremy puts a hand on my shoulder. "Did someone do something immoral in here while I wasn't looking?" Jeremy doesn't even laugh at his own joke.

"Will you call me a taxi, please? I can't stay here. I need to go home. I'll collect my car tomorrow."

Jeremy spins me around and looks at me intently. "Are you sure?"

All I have in me is a quick nod.

# CHAPTER FIFTEEN

● ● ● ● ● ● ● ● ● ● ● ● ● ● ● ● ● ●

I try to unlock Dolores' door as quietly as possible. It takes a few seconds before I remember the code for the alarm, but I manage to punch it in, anyway—it's the numbers that make up Ian's birthday: 17061981.

*Oh shit*, his birthday is in less than three weeks. The sudden realization makes me stand with my hands against the door for a minute, catching my breath.

I'm too drunk to do this gracefully, I think, when I head up the stairs to Dolores' room—our room. I don't always use the guest bathroom anymore, but tonight I do. I shed my clothes, leaving them in an untidy pile on the bathroom floor, and only bother to put on my pajama top. It's getting warmer. We'll have to switch on the air conditioning in the bedroom soon. I forego brushing my teeth and tip-toe to the bedroom.

The TV is still on, but paused on the Netflix home screen, casting a sleeping Dolores in a gaudy sort of light. I'm glad for the illumination so I don't wake her with my stumbling in the dark at this ungodly hour. I'm not sure whether I'm glad she managed to go to sleep without me, but then, when I take a closer look at her peaceful sleeping face, I am. A warm glow spreads through me at the sight of her. Then I see the bottle of Ambien on her night stand. I can guess where she got that.

Figuring I no longer have to be ultra-quiet, I walk to my side of the bed, sit on the edge and switch off the TV. The Ambien must have knocked her out really well, because Dolores is lying in the middle of the bed and, despite it being a generous king-size, she's not leaving me a lot of room. But I didn't come back here for a lot of space in bed. In fact, I rushed over here in a taxi in the middle of the night because I wanted the opposite.

Dolores is lying on her back and I sidle up to her, wrapping an arm around her middle. Her tank top has ridden up and my arm is on her bare, warm skin. I put my head in the crook of her shoulder, enveloping her as much as I can. Then extreme fatigue hits me right on the head, and I nod off in minutes—minutes of sweet bliss for having someone to come home to, someone who warmed up the bed for me.

* * *

I don't know what time it is when I wake up, but my head is pounding like someone has taken a hammer to it. I'm lying in a puddle of my own sweat, which is no wonder because Dolores is perched half on top of me. It's only when I come to a little more that I realize one of her hands is tucked underneath my pajama top, her hot palm on my belly. It's a touch so intimate—so foreign to me by now—that I break out into even more of a hot flash.

I want to get out from underneath Dolores. Her breath is in my ear. Her hand rises and falls with my own breath, quickening as my pulse picks up speed. What is this? I truly ask myself for the first time. What are we doing here? What am I still doing here? I can really only begin my life again once I move out of Dolores' house, but the mere thought of it frightens me to such an extent that I find her hand underneath my top, and clasp it in mine.

I turn to look at Dolores. Early light is already coming through the blinds and I can make out her wrinkles, a freckle next to her nose, an unevenness underneath her temple.

I have the rest of my life to learn to be alone again. There's no way I'm leaving Dolores' house. How would I cope with the same sheer panic that gripped me when I walked into Jeremy's guest room, or the prospect of waking up alone and wanting Ian beside me so much it physically hurts. Where would I even go?

The bottle of Ambien looks very tempting, but the alarm clock on Dolores' side of the bed shows six already. I consider sleeping it off, just taking a day off from this grief, but I don't want to disturb Dolores by moving. Her closeness calms me, even takes the sting off that pulsating headache at the back of my skull. Glancing at her relaxed features relaxes me in turn.

I bring an arm to her back and pull her a little closer. I lie like this for a long time, trying to focus on my breath, and on the feel of someone else's skin on mine.

* * *

I wake up again when Dolores starts to move. When I open my eyes, I stare straight into hers. Her hand is still on my belly, mine is still on her back. We haven't moved an inch since I fell back asleep.

"Hey," she whispers, but doesn't move away, "you're here."

"Yeah," I whisper back, not wanting to disturb the peaceful morning atmosphere.

"I'm glad." She must only then notice where her hand is because she looks down at my belly. "Oh." She retracts it immediately. "I'm sorry about that." She gives a small, apologetic smile.

"It's okay." With that, the moment has passed.

She rolls away, putting a few inches of distance between us, and pulls her top all the way down. "I couldn't sleep, so I took one of your pills. I hope you don't mind."

I shake my head while I bring my hands to my face and massage my temples.

"How was the party? Rough night?"

I'm relieved she doesn't ask why I came back. She doesn't need to. She knows. Just as I know why she went against her own advice and took a pill on the one night I wasn't here. Some things are better left unsaid.

"I drank too much." I give an exaggerated moan. "Jeremy has a very heavy hand when it comes to pouring champagne."

My head is thrown back on the pillow so I only hear the chuckle Dolores produces. "But you had a good time?"

"Hm," I grunt. "It was good to see my friends." I tell her about Alex's pregnancy and how Ethan, whom Dolores has known since Ian was in high school, still hasn't cut his hair, and we chit chat for a couple of minutes, I bringing her up to speed on Ian's friends' lives, she listening attentively, not caring that her hair is all over the place, and there are tiny crusts in the corners of her eyes, and the shoulder band of her tank top has slipped down. Dolores just listens.

"What do you want to do today?" she asks, after I'm done talking.

Simply being asked the question fills me with the same warm glow I felt when I entered the bedroom last night.

"Sleep some more. Be brought breakfast in bed. Get a head and shoulder massage. Become an alcoholic and repeat all of that tomorrow." I make my voice drip with pathos.

"Some of those things can be arranged, some I would advise against." She smiles broadly and it feels as though the brightness of her smile clears some more of my headache. "Why don't we go see a movie instead? It'll get us out of the house. We can go out to dinner after."

"Didn't you have that thing this afternoon?" Dolores always has so many plans, I can't keep up, but I distinctly remember her telling me that she would be out this afternoon.

"I cancelled last night. I wasn't very interested in seeing that play, anyway. And matinees aren't really my thing. I don't like the sort of crowd it draws."

"Snobbish, much?" I joke in a way I usually wouldn't with Dolores.

She still has a soft smile on her face. "I have standards, that's all."

Silence falls and we both just keep lying there. I'm aware of the extreme intimacy of these minutes we've just spent chatting in bed. It's precious and healing and makes me feel like a human being again.

"Which art house movie would Lady Flemming like to see?" I turn on my side and look her straight in the face.

"Something with subtitles, obviously."

"Obviously."

We mirror smiles at each other and, as the sun beams brightly into the bedroom, illuminating Dolores from behind, a short silence descends again, and I feel something has changed between us. This joking. This lingering in bed. It's deeper than the grief we shared initially. There's a charge in the air. It's in her smile, but also in mine. Our smiles are real, coming from an unexpected place of joy, no matter how fleeting or flimsy, within us. Perhaps we're both acknowledging, at the same time, that, together, we can find a way out of this dread.

Dolores raises her hand and pushes a stray strand of hair away from my face. "I missed you," she whispers, her voice barely audible. "More than I thought I would." Her fingers linger close to my cheek, then she brushes them against my skin.

I push my cheek against her fingers, wanting to feel more of her touch. "I missed you too." The words barely make it out of my throat. I have no idea what's going on here, what to make of this. My right hand glides to her belly, my fingers grab for her top. And in a moment where I lose complete control of my faculties, I pull her close, bring my hand underneath her tank top, feel the hot skin of her belly against my fingers, her hand against my cheek, and I kiss her full on the lips.

I don't know why. It's not something I've ever considered for a split second of my life. It just happens, as a result of this moment, and the ones we've been having before. One minute we're just talking, the next I'm kissing her.

When my mind takes over again from whatever had seized control of my senses, I pull back. "Oh fuck, I'm so sorry. I—I really didn't—" I stammer, but I can't move. Dolores is still so close, her skin radiating its heat onto mine.

"It's okay. There's no one here to judge you, Sophie." She brings her thumb to my jaw and just leaves it there, not breaking contact.

Then I burst out laughing. "Jesus, Dolores. I must still be drunk." I pull away from her completely, ending this moment of insanity. "I don't know what came over me." I throw the covers off me, but she grabs my hand.

"We can talk about this. It doesn't have to be something more than it is."

"I'd better get up." Flustered, because I have no idea what's happening to me—all I know is that I need to get out of this room—I jump out of bed and hurry to the guest bedroom. I crash down onto the bed, dazed, trying to figure out what just happened.

I kissed Dolores.

# CHAPTER SIXTEEN

●●●●●●●●●●●●●●●●●●●

After I've taken a shower and calmed myself down, I sit at my desk. I pull the folder in which I keep my letters to Ian from a drawer and stare at them. But all I can really think of is my lips on Dolores'. The soft familiarity of them, the ease with which I pulled her close, as though it had been in the stars since that first night I ended up in her bed. What must she think of me now? That I've wanted to kiss her all along, while that couldn't be further removed from the truth. And what did she imply when she said it didn't have to be anything more than it was? Oh fuck. I'm going to have to talk to her. But what can I possibly say in my defense?

I look up and see my reflection in the computer screen. "She's right, Sophie," I tell myself. "It doesn't mean anything. It was just grief expressing itself in another way. Pull yourself together."

By the time I make it downstairs, Dolores is fully dressed and made-up. On Sundays she doesn't primp herself up as much as on other days. She's wearing jeans and a pink linen blouse. She sits at the kitchen table, reading *The Post* with her glasses on.

"Your mother is one of the most stunning women I've ever met," I said to Ian once, after which he gave me a funny look, though I could tell there was a sense of pride in his glance as well.

Looking at Dolores now, I can hear myself say those words to him again. It's not a beauty that has its root in the brands of make-up she uses and how, or in the expensive clothes she wears, it comes from inside of her. I know this for certain now because she looked just as beautiful in bed this morning. Why else would I have kissed her?

Dolores looks up over the thick rim of her glasses. "Breakfast?" she asks, as though I didn't just kiss her.

I ignore her question. "I want to apologize for my behavior, Dolores. I have no idea what came over me, but I don't want anything to change between us." Though I can hardly expect her to let me back into her bed after the stunt I just pulled. "Can we please pretend it never happened? I had a very emotional night. I'm sure there's some psychological explanation for it, but I'd rather not dwell on it."

"Calm down, Sophie." She takes off her glasses. "Sit down. Have some coffee." She points to the place she set for me at the breakfast table, and it's these little things, the small pieces of evidence of what she does for me, how she takes care of me, how she's there for me in minor day-to-day things, that has helped me the most. What a fool I am to jeopardize that.

I sit and concentrate on pouring myself a cup of coffee. When I drink, I look her straight in the eyes.

"Don't feel bad about what happened," Dolores says. "If I recall correctly, I woke up with my body draped all over yours. We're two human beings sharing a bed. These things happen."

I put down my cup. "I wouldn't want you to think that I have any ulterior motives for sleeping in your bed. The only reason is that I can't face sleeping alone. Not just yet."

"Oh, honey, of course I don't think that." She half-smiles.

"Do you, er, think this has been going on for too long? Us sleeping together?"

"Do *you*?" Dolores sounds a little offended, or maybe it's just my imagination playing tricks on me. I really shouldn't trust my brain, or my body, today.

"I don't know. I can't sleep in your bed forever." I repeat Jeremy's words from the other day, after which I recall the dread I felt when I merely stood at the threshold of his guest bedroom, at the thought of sleeping alone—as though sleeping has become this symbol for my grieving process. As though it has become the most telling part of the aftermath of Ian's death.

"That would be a little strange, admittedly." Dolores shoves her newspaper aside and reaches for my hand. I let her grab it. "Why don't we say what this is really about? I'll start, okay?"

Taken aback, I nod. I thought I was doing a pretty good job of trying to explain myself, even though I don't have that much to say because of temporary insanity and such things.

"I won't claim that what happened is perfectly normal, because for us, perfectly normal doesn't exist anymore. Our entire world has been torn down in a flash and all we're trying to do is make our way out from underneath the rubble. That's it. By any means possible. What we're doing now is merely surviving, until we can manage to find some pleasure and meaning in this life again. Which may take a while, months, years, decades. Who knows? But if a kiss can make you feel a little bit like your old self again, a little more human, a little more than the survivor you are now, then I'll kiss you every day." She pauses, starts to say something, then swallows her words.

While I find comfort in her words, and feel a little less ill at ease, I'm ashamed for the thought that makes its way to the forefront of my brain. *But you're a lesbian, Dolores. I'm not.* I imagine that's not the kind of straight-talking she had in mind.

"Whatever it takes," I say, while I feel my cheeks flush.

"Now will you go to the movies with me this afternoon?" she asks.

"On a date, you mean?" My lips curve into a smile.

Dolores huffs out a chuckle. "Whatever it takes," she says.

*** 

*Ian,*

*You're not going to believe this. I kissed your mother. I know. Please don't judge. Oh, okay. You can judge. You should. I deserve it. We have this precious, fragile thing going on between us. This balance that we managed to find amidst all this loss and grief. I keep calling it comfort, but I guess it's more than that. When you sleep in someone's bed for more than two months, it has to be more than that.*

*I just haven't been willing to let my mind go there, Ian. She's your mother. The fact that she's a lesbian hasn't suddenly escaped me either. Not that it would be so different if she were straight. I don't know. This morning I felt so mortified, but less so now. It's in the way she says things. Dolores is the most nonjudgmental person I've ever met. She was always like that with you as well. I clearly remember that. She never said "I told you so," but allowed you to make your own mistakes and learn at your own pace, and never gloated.*

*We're going to the movies later. Just Dolores and I. Do you find that strange? I think Jeremy is beginning to find it strange, or at least very uncommon. But you know what? I wouldn't be staying at your mother's house, sleeping in her bed, if you were still alive, Ian. Goddamn it.*

*Last night, I went to a party at Jeremy's and, just for a brief moment, I was so angry because you weren't there. Not long after, I rushed back to Dolores. You know she advised me to see someone, a shrink. Maybe I should see someone. Dolores and I are so intertwined in this. Grief defines us. It's all we are, together. That's how it feels sometimes.*

*Can you tell I'm terribly hungover?*

*This letter is going nowhere… but there's one last thought I want to express. I know Dolores is not your biological mother, but to my great surprise, now that you're no longer here, I recognize so much of you in her. It's in the details. All the small things she does for me, the way you did. All the little actions you deemed normal for two people who loved each other to do for one another. A thoughtfulness I never really knew before I met you, and that I hoped has rubbed off on me a little.*

*She spoils me. You spoiled me too, Ian. Most people wouldn't even see it that way, but I do. She buys things for me in the grocery store that she would never eat herself, like Nutella and peanut butter and cheese she finds bland. In the morning, before she goes to work—because unlike me, your mother has gone back to work—she lays out all the breakfast things for me, the way you used to do.*

*I guess if I'm really being honest with myself, I can kind of see what I'm doing here. I'm replacing you with her. We have dinner together. We watch TV together. Go to bed and wake up together. You know I was never very good at being alone for long stretches of time. In that, I have found the perfect companion in Dolores.*

*Fuck, this is weird.*

*I would apologize for telling you all of this, but you're dead, and that's the only reason why I'm even staying here.*

*So, you'll have to excuse me, Ian, but I have to get ready for my date with your mother now.*

*I miss you—although really, those three words can never truly convey what it feels like to have someone brutally ripped out of your life the way you have been. I feel like half a person, like only a part of me remains, and not the very good part.*

*Love, always,*

*Sophie*

\* \* \*

After the movie, which I was unable to focus on for more than three consecutive minutes, Dolores takes me to a tiny restaurant that I've never been to before, let alone knew existed, not far from her house. It's run by a tubby Italian woman, whose husband is the chef.

"I'm glad you're eating again. I was worried about you for a while," Dolores says.

I devour the thin slices of the pizza we've decided to share. "A hangover will do that to you."

"Dessert?" she asks.

"Why the hell not?" I'm feeling a little reckless tonight.

Or perhaps it's the effect of the half bottle of red we've shared. After only one gulp, it seemed to re-instate that early buzz I'd felt last night after two glasses of champagne. The tipping point between tipsy and well-on-the-way-to-drunk. That hazy feeling that settles in your brain and makes everything so much more bearable. When I glance at Dolores' glass I see she's barely touched her wine.

Dolores calls over the owner, whom she calls by her first name, Maria, and asks what's for dessert today. We have the choice between panna cotta and tiramisu.

"We'll have one of each," Dolores says, without consulting me.

"And I'll have an Amaretto, no ice," I add.

"Make that two," Dolores says. "We can walk home. It's a beautiful evening."

"Do you feel responsible for me?" I ask, once Maria has headed to the bar. I surprise myself with the question, but I guess I'm too tired, emotionally and physically, to rely on any filter for thoughts that pop up randomly in my brain.

"How do you mean?" Dolores rests her chin on her fist and regards me intently.

"You watch my eating habits. You make me breakfast. You offered me a place to stay."

Dolores averts her gaze for a second, then looks at me again. "Not so much responsible, although I do worry about you. I think that's only natural. But, and I'm guessing this might be mutual, you're all I have left of him. You shared a life with him. Being around you makes me feel as though a little part of him is still around as well."

I couldn't have said it more eloquently myself. I don't know if I was being flippant earlier, or what I was even trying to get out of asking her, but her easy reply has reinforced the rapport between us.

"I write him letters. Every day. Sometimes a few per day. Letters he will never read, but it helps to gather my thoughts, to give them a place."

Dolores nods. "That's good."

Maria brings over the desserts and drinks and while she arranges everything on the table, I think of how that kiss this morning has torn down the last remaining wall between Dolores and me. The letters are something I would only discuss with Jeremy, my best friend, but now I've told Dolores, bringing us even closer.

"I talk to him," Dolores confesses after Maria has left. "Every chance I get. In the car. When I'm alone in my office. When I'm getting dressed. I deliberately stop what I'm doing and I tell him about my day, about a new artist we'll be showing at the gallery, or just what I had for lunch, the way I used to." She delves a spoon into the panna cotta and, to my surprise, brings it to my mouth. "Come on, Sophie. Open wide." She follows up with a sad smile, the kind that tries to be bright and encouraging but just can't get there because there's no sparkle in its bearer's eyes.

I open my mouth and let Dolores feed me a spoonful of dessert.

# CHAPTER SEVENTEEN

●●●●●●●●●●●●●●●●●●●

When we go upstairs to sleep, Dolores shows no sign that I'm not welcome in her bed anymore. I don't ask her because, although I could try the guest room, I already know I would either resort to Ambien, or crawl back into her bed in the middle of the night. I'm spent, having not eliminated all remnants of my hangover. I'm feeling extra tender because of our conversation at dinner, and a little misty-eyed because of too much Amaretto and lowered inhibitions.

As though nothing happened in the very same bed that morning, we both hop in. When Dolores offers her arm for me to lay my head upon, it does feel as though we've spent this Sunday as much more than two women bound together by the dead man they loved. Dolores and I are friends now. She's the one I'm closest to now that Ian is dead. What started as shared grief has morphed into an enormous amount of respect and tenderness for this woman I was always a teensy bit afraid of, in the way most people are intimidated by their partner's parents. And look at me now, I think, as I sink into Dolores' comforting embrace.

She flicks through some channels, soon declaring there's nothing on. We've watched all *Grace & Frankie* episodes on Netflix and haven't started anything new yet.

"Shall I just switch it off?" Dolores asks, one hand on the remote, the other in my hair, stroking my scalp so softly, so gently, it lulls me into a different state of being. The state I was in this morning when I put my hand on her belly, when her fingers stroked my cheek, and I planted my lips onto hers.

I'm too tired, too under the influence of grief, alcohol, and affection to give much thought to it. I'm just relieved to be feeling something else than the relentless dull ache of loss that beats inside me like a second heart, and seems so endless, so impossible to overcome, that I just give in to the impulse to bring my hand back to Dolores' belly, and trace a finger underneath the hem of her tank top. I cease to have any thoughts entirely when my fingers crawl higher underneath her top. Dolores' muscles don't stiffen. She just lies there while I stroke the soft, soft skin of her belly, touch the heat of it. She switches off the television, bathing the room in welcome darkness.

I trace a finger around her belly button, let it dip in, then out again, and push her top higher with the back of my hand. Her skin is pale but smooth and so incredibly soft, I long to lose myself in its entire expanse, long to lose every little part of me that hurts so much.

Dolores' hand is still in my hair, but slowly creeps down to my neck, where she traces her fingertips along the collar of my pajama top. This is not a level of touching we're accustomed to; it's brand new, stirring up something deep inside of me, something I thought had disappeared with Ian's death. Something I don't want to name, only feel.

"Sophie," she whispers then, and I recognize the urgency in the low whimper of her voice. It reflects the tremor that has started beneath my flesh. This course of action that started with a touch of my finger against her belly, and has now, so it seems, become irreversible. I don't want to pull away. In fact, pulling away from Dolores is the very last thing I ever want to do. I've lost so much already.

I leave my hand where it is while I push my face away from her shoulder and crane my neck to look at her. I don't say anything. I'm not sure about what exactly is going to happen, but I do know that, whatever it is, it needs to happen in silence, in an atmosphere of solemnness and inevitability. It's the only way. And it's what I want. My eyes have grown accustomed to the dark and, this time, when I look into Dolores' eyes, they do sparkle.

I could spend a few seconds deciphering that look on her face, but I don't want to. I just want to progress, put some things behind me, become someone else, if even for fifteen minutes. I want to forget.

I push myself up, find a fragile sort of balance, with my hand now on Dolores' hipbone and my left arm awkwardly bent, elbow thrust into a pillow. *Why not?* Is the only thought running through my head as I inch my mouth closer to Dolores'. Why the hell not? Because maybe this isn't supposed to happen, but so are many other things. Like Ian cycling along Paterson Street at the exact moment that truck started reversing, losing his balance, and cracking his skull on the sidewalk.

If I live in a world where such a coincidental atrocity can take place, then so can this. It's not the opposite, it won't even things out—because what's the opposite of death? It's not life. I've learned that in the past two months. Yes, my heart is still beating, the bones of my skull are intact, but I sure as hell haven't been feeling alive. Except now, when my lips hover so close to Dolores' mouth that I can smell the Amaretto on her breath. It's the most alive I've felt since it happened.

I know this needs to come from me. I need to initiate. I need to kiss her, lay my hand on her skin. It can't be the other way around because then it would mean something else. But when my lips finally touch hers, I know it's right. In my universe and in this moment, on this wretched Sunday evening, the tenth without Ian, I'm kissing his mother in her bed, and for the very first time, it's not just grief pulsing underneath my skin, it's this other thing, this thing I've been feeling for Dolores that is reaching its apex, but I can't define just yet.

The kiss is tentative, close-lipped, inquiring. But already it feels entirely different than this morning's kiss.

This time, when I kiss her, it's not an accident. All my intention is behind it, all this pain I don't want to feel anymore. It's all there, on the surface of my lips, when they meet hers. And again, our mouths a little wider this time, exchanging breath. When our lips touch next, I let the tip of my tongue slip in, just to test the waters. When I feel Dolores' tongue meet mine I see it as being given permission. Permission for my tongue to further its claim on her mouth, but also permission to give in to the heat that is building in my stomach, to surrender to all these emotions pent-up in my flesh.

There's lust in our kiss, a desire to extinguish and take from the other—I certainly want to take whatever I can get from Dolores, even if it's just a couple of minutes of complete solace—but there's also tenderness, a reflection of how fond I've grown of Dolores. Of her elegant ways, her backbone made of iron. Even though she cracks sometimes, she's still the strongest person I've ever met.

When I kiss Dolores, and my tongue darts in and out of her mouth, I don't think of Ian. Even though this kiss is the direct result of him dying, this kiss has, in its essence, nothing to do with Ian. This is about Dolores and me. The twosome we've formed in mourning. The unlikely bedfellows we've become. The alliance we've created against our grief when it was at its earliest and sharpest. It's us versus everything else.

Only when Dolores brings both her hands behind my neck, do I allow myself to slip on top of her. I glance down at her but then quickly close my eyes again, and kiss her. I kiss and kiss her, until everything inside me mellows, my skin melts into hers, until her mouth on mine is all I feel. Until I'm no longer grieving Sophie, but Sophie so full of desire for another person, I lose myself completely.

I'm not sure how long we've been kissing when Dolores pulls back a little. It's not the sort of flinching away that indicates a sudden change of heart or rejection, but a pause. Dolores looks at me while she sucks her bottom lip into her mouth, as though she wants to taste the remnants of our kisses. And it's strange because her lips don't curve into a smile, but it feels as though she's smiling at me, encouraging me, telling me something with a facial expression that isn't even there. This is how things have evolved between us. I understand Dolores in a way I've never understood anyone in my life. I feel what she feels. I want what she wants. I suddenly know what cosmic alignment feels like, even though I've never even thought of that concept a single time in my life.

Dolores slips from underneath me and pushes herself up to a half-sitting position. She brings her hands behind my neck and kisses me again and while she does, she pushes me down onto my back, until she's the one lying on top of me. Instantly, it feels different. More heated. More fire lighting up under the surface of my skin. For the first time, I wonder what she'll do next, because her weight on top of me tells me something else: this is Dolores' house, Dolores' bedroom, and she's in charge here. It's how I want it, oh so much. For her to let me do this—let us do this—but to take the reins from me. To take responsibility.

*Do whatever you want with me*, I want to scream. *I'm all yours. Every last fiber of my being belongs to you right now. I want you.*

I want Dolores.

She slides half off me and, slowly, starts unbuttoning my pajama top. She brushes the sides away and fixes her eyes on my chest. Her stare is soon followed by a fingertip brushing against my skin, in between my breasts. It's only when her finger reaches one of my nipples, hardening it beyond belief, that it hits me that we're really doing this. A fresh pang of lust burrows its way through my flesh. Even though I can't in good conscience lie here, underneath Dolores' increasingly insistent touch, and claim that I've dreamed about a night like this for a long time, it doesn't come as a surprise either. It feels more like a natural, logical progression of two women sleeping in the same bed for so long.

Dolores circles my nipple with her fingertip, and I seem to feel her gaze on me as much as her touch. When she leans in and traces her tongue around my nipple in a circle, the exact same way her finger did a second earlier, something lets loose inside of me. Perhaps the last ounce of inhibition I had left in me. I bring one hand into her hair, and one to her back, underneath her top, and a moan escapes me. I'm already so lit up for her, so fiery, so ready.

She focuses on my other nipple, expanding the reach of her tongue, then kissing her way to my throat, where her thumb rests against the hollow of it.

I start hoisting up her top, even though I know I can't get it off her like that, but I'm so overcome with desire to shed all that stands between us now. Our clothes have to go pronto. I want to keep this delicious momentum going, this string of explosions in my flesh, this complete erasure of what's been going on in my life. I want all of Dolores, all of her skin against mine, all of her inside of me.

Dolores catches my drift. She pushes herself away from me briefly and in one fluid motion pulls her tank top over her head and bares her chest to me. My pulse picks up speed at the sight of her, because this really is the point of no return. I shrug out of my pajama top and start pushing my pants down, but Dolores puts her hands on me, calming me. She gives me a look I've never seen before, perhaps not on anyone, and I give her control over my further disrobing.

She hooks her fingers underneath the waistband and slides my pajama bottoms down, until I'm lying in front of her in just a pair of flimsy panties. I glance at her, see her swallow hard. From what I'm seeing, what we're doing is turning her on greatly. When she looks at me there's nothing but intent in her glance, total focus. It doesn't even matter whether she's doing this for me, or for her, or for us. None of it matters. Yes, we're having sex, consensual, all-the-way sex, but this is so much more than two bodies meeting physically. I know she knows. We're still aligned. In fact, my desire is aligned with Dolores' so much, that the sight of her lust spurs mine on even more. I can't explain why my body reacts this way to her touch, but it does. Oh, it does.

Underneath my panties, I'm alive as I've ever been. My pussy lips throb and pulse as though there's no tomorrow—maybe, for that particular part of my body, there is none.

Dolores trails her finger along the waistband of my panties, leaving an expanse of goosebumps in its wake. I want that damned piece of fabric off me, but, somehow, I know to let her guide this, to let her lead me into whatever comes next.

My breath is coming in short gusts and my brain is dominated by a lust so pure, so focused, I fear there might be part of me missing after this is over. Or maybe that's what I'm secretly hoping for. I want to disappear. Lose myself in this moment, in Dolores' exquisite touch, in her love for me—because I have no doubt she loves me, and I love her right back.

Her finger travels south now, over the fabric of my panties. She strokes my lips and I offer myself a little more to her. I buck up my hips, wanting to make my desire as clear as possible, though at this point there's no more chance of being misunderstood.

Her fingers skate up and down and the sensation is so divine, so full of promise, I huff out a moan again. All this softness, this delicate dedication to me, is not missing its effect. I want to beg her, but what we are doing here tonight, needs to remain as wordless as possible. No talk, just action. Affection. Emotion. Pleasure.

Pleasure.

The very thing that seemed the most unattainable and which I'm luxuriously bathing in now.

My esteem for Dolores only grows as her fingertips

finally curve underneath my panties and she starts tugging them down. She is a woman free of prudishness, of guilt, of anything that might stop her from doing this.

When my pussy meets the air, the engine that's been steadily humming inside of me is revved up another notch. Every nerve ending in my body stands to attention as Dolores sidles up to me, flanks my side with the warmth of her body and, at last, traces a finger along my bare, wet lips. She's perched up on one arm, looking at me, ready to enter me.

Then she does. She slides inside of me. Slowly, deliberately, gauging. And that's when I truly disappear. There's no more pain in my world. No more loss. Only Dolores' finger inside of me. When she slips out and adds another, slowly stroking me, I throw my head back into the pillows, bare my neck to her. She kisses me just below the ear and I can hear her breath, her arousal in it.

Dolores' fingers thrust high and deep inside of me, fill me, and empty me at the same time. Every time she delivers another thrust, some of the pent-up tension flees my muscles, a morsel of pain gets unstuck from where it has lodged itself deep inside of me. The longer she fucks me, the more I lose myself, but the more I become myself again. But even in those moments of sweet bliss, of divine physical sensation, I know that this feeling won't last. That it's fleeting. Glorious, but passing. A short bout of relief. A reprieve from my doomed reality. Maybe that's why I seem to feel her fingers everywhere.

Those kisses she's planting on the sensitive skin of my neck pierce all the way down to my soul. A layer of sweat forms where her body meets mine, the hairs on the back of my neck stand up as she fucks me, her fingers curling inside of me, taking me, stealing from me what I'm so desperate to lose. This second skin I've grown since Ian's death. This armor around my heart. It all comes crumbling down as she hits that spot inside me, repeatedly, and she coaxes from me a pleasure so base, so animalistic, that the world seems to cave in around me as a climax washes over me, starting from somewhere deep inside of me, the place where I've been holding all my pain. As I climax, losing control over my muscles for an instant, stepping out of my body while pure pleasure takes over, I let out a guttural groan, one straight from the heart, tears rolling down my cheeks.

Dolores gently slips her fingers out and as soon as I'm empty of her—because that's how it feels—I want her again. I can't stop my tears from falling. They're coming out in big, heaving gulps now. I haven't cried that much anymore the past few weeks, and it's as though my body wants to make up for that now. As though it's trying to say that I still have a shitload of grieving to do, no matter how exquisitely I let Ian's mother fuck me.

"It's okay," Dolores' whispers. She's still flanking me. The hand with which she fucked me on my cheek, her thumb stroking me. "Let it all out."

She holds me while I cry, until my tear ducts run dry, and I feel raw and empty and sated.

"I'm sorry." I'm not really apologizing. It's more something automatic coming from my mouth as I wipe some of the tears from my cheeks.

"Don't ever say sorry for crying." Dolores kisses me on the cheek.

"I don't really know what else to say." I manage a bit of a chuckle.

"How do you feel?" she whispers.

I turn on my side, facing her. "Like I owe you something." I give her a quick smile before pressing my lips to hers.

She puts both her hands on my cheeks and pulls away from me a bit. "Sophie, please, you don't owe me anything."

"I do owe you this." I bring a hand to her belly, the way I did before, when I started all of this, but it's not the same anymore. Most of the fire inside of me has been extinguished. Though I can hardly consider that fair.

Dolores reaches for my hand, presses it against her body. "You don't." Her tone is insistent. "Not now."

*Not now?* Does that imply she's expecting us to do this again?

"I just thought... I—" I have no idea what I'm supposed to say.

"I know what you're thinking." Dolores' voice is buttery soft. "But it's okay. I promise you. It's more than okay."

I decide to let it go, following Dolores' lead—again. "For what it's worth, and despite that river of tears, I really, truly enjoyed that." I can't keep a hint of bashfulness out of my voice. Because we can't go back anymore now. After that quick kiss this morning, it was almost ridiculously easy to pretend it didn't happen. However, knowing what I know now, the memory of it must have been doing some work in the background of my mind. We slept together in the other sense of the expression. Dolores' fingers were inside of me. She made me come so hard I howled, the echo of my scream still reverberating somewhere in the house.

"I know." She kisses me on the tip of my nose, almost innocently.

"Where do we go from here?"

"To sleep would be my suggestion," she says matter-of-factly.

I feel myself mellowing again, recovering from the shock of orgasm and the subsequent onslaught of tears. I melt into Dolores' embrace a little more. Why does life feel so much more bearable in her arms? The world like not such a hopeless place?

"What about when we wake up?" I whisper. My body is exhausted by the shedding of tension, but I'm not sleepy. My brain is too alert, trying to process too much.

"When we wake up, we'll take a shower. Then we'll see."

"We'll need to talk about this in the cold hard light of day."

"Only if we want to."

"There's just some things I want you to know. I didn't crawl into bed with you tonight with what just happened as the outcome I was hoping for. I had no such intention. It just… happened. However lame that sounds."

"Tell me this, Sophie. Did you enjoy it?"

"Yes, of course, but—"

"No buts. It's too late for buts. Or for any other negative emotion you might experience. This is something that happened between us. Something that made us feel good. Something that will help us sleep at night. Try looking at it from the bright side." She presses her lips to my scalp.

*Try looking at it from the bright side.* An expression so quintessentially Ian's, it makes the hairs on the back of my neck stand up.

"I'll try." It's easy when I'm ensconced in Dolores' loving embrace.

"I have an early day tomorrow. We're setting up a new show and I need to be there when the pieces arrive. Will you be all right on your own? You're welcome to join me. We can always use an extra pair of hands at the gallery when it's set-up time."

Ian loved going to his mother's galleries when new pieces had just arrived. He'd often leave work early and give Dolores and her staff a hand.

"What time does the alarm go off?"

"Six," Dolores says.

"You may have to use force to get me out of bed, but yes, I'd like to go with you." I already have no clue how I'll catch any sleep tonight, how I'll silence the stream of new thoughts coming my way after what just happened. There's no way I'm staying home alone here all day tomorrow, working on what's supposed to become a novel, but is really just me fretting about everything under the guise of trying something new. Being out of the house will do me good. Using my hands will do me good. I'm suddenly flattered that Dolores asked.

"I'll use my imagination to get you out," she says, a chuckle lurking under the breathiness of her voice.

# CHAPTER EIGHTEEN

● ● ● ● ● ● ● ● ● ● ● ● ● ● ● ● ● ● ●

"Sophie," Dolores whispers. "Do you want to get up with me?"

When I open my eyes, for the very first time my initial thought upon waking is not that Ian is dead, but that I slept with his mother. *Oh fuck.*

"Er, yes," I murmur, because I need to get out of that bed pronto.

My body is still exhausted, but my mind is instantly wide awake. Memories of last night assault me. I was the one who started it. I was the one who put my hand on her belly. How can I possibly face Dolores—and myself in the mirror?

I jump out of bed and just stand there in the dark for a while, not knowing what to do, so thrown by my own actions, by being in this bedroom, which has been such a place of comfort and which I have now made into something else entirely. Did I really agree to spend the day with Dolores? I would have last night, while under the influence of a, frankly, mind-blowing orgasm. Dolores watched me climax. She *made* me climax. Ian's death has really fucked me up well and good.

"Do you want to shower first?" Dolores asks.

Only then do I realize I'm standing in her bedroom fully naked. Dolores is still wearing her tank top, and her underwear for that matter, while my garments are spread about the room, like a filthy—guilty—reminder of what happened here last night.

"I'll use the other bathroom." I don't say anything else, just hurry out of the room.

When I reach the guest bathroom, I don't look in the mirror, but hop straight into a spray of scalding hot water, as if the hotter it is, the more it can wash away what happened. Because none of this, not a single second of it, can be construed as acceptable. I can't even write this to Ian in a letter he will never read.

There's no way I'm going to the gallery with Dolores.

I stand under the cascading water for long minutes, scrubbing my skin raw and, eventually, putting my hands against the wall to catch my breath because my motions have been too frantic. It's too early, I didn't get enough sleep. Ian is dead. I slept with his mother. Well, not technically his mother. Oh yes, I'm making the distinction now, even though Ian never did.

I asked him once whether he considered Dolores less of a mother to him than Angela, who had given birth to him, who shared DNA with him. Ian got so offended by that, claiming that, even though Dolores had never been able to legally adopt him—because, on paper, Ian always had two parents—she'd been a million times more a parent to him than his biological father, who didn't care about him enough to not move to England shortly after the divorce, when Ian was only five years old.

Right at this minute though, I'm finding it, for the very first time, terribly convenient that Angela and Dolores never married. But as I turn off the tap and inhale gulp after gulp of steam, I know that a piece of paper doesn't make a difference.

I slept with Ian's mother. It's as dreadfully simple as that.

"Sophie?" Dolores says. She's standing in the doorframe of the guest room when I exit the bathroom. "Do you want breakfast? We can grab something next door to the gallery later if you don't feel like it now."

How can she even speak to me like this? Like nothing happened? How can she expect me to spend the day with her? Or is this what lesbians do?

"I don't think I will join you after all, Dolores. I'm sorry. I don't mean to hold you up. You go on without me." I somehow manage to make my voice sound even and free of tremors. I wrap the towel tightly around me—as though she hasn't seen, and felt, all of me yet.

"Are you sure?" She gives me a funny look. "Will you be all right on your own all day?"

"Yes. No." The stammering begins. "I should probably move out. I've been here long enough. This is all wrong."

"You're freaking out. I understand. Just... don't do anything rash. Let's meet for lunch. I can come home or we can meet wherever you want. Let's talk first."

How can she be so calm about this when she had her fingers inside of me last night?

"Okay." I just want her out of this room, out of my sight. I don't want to be reminded of what she has let me become. A pervert. Someone who degraded the memory of her dead partner by sleeping with his mother. A harlot.

"Sophie." Dolores' voice has lowered to a whisper again. "Please remember, it was just sex." She gives me a slight nod, then walks out of the room.

I start to shiver. My skin is still partially wet. I close the door, wrap the towel around me more tightly, almost cutting off my breath, and crawl into bed. The bed I should have been sleeping in all along. I wait until the noises downstairs die down and I hear the front door shut with a little bang.

Once I'm alone in the house, and I feel as though I can start breathing again, I get dressed and sit at my desk. What the hell am I going to do? Maybe I should write my novel about this. About a grief so obliterating it crushes all common sense. Then my stomach starts growling. I'm appalled that my body could even experience something as mundane as hunger right now. And I'm reminded of what Dolores said to me last night over dinner. That she was glad I was eating again. Dolores, whose kindness lulled me into a state in which I'm capable of instigating sex with her. I can't deal with this alone. I need to talk to Jeremy. I need someone to judge me, because having to do it on my own doesn't seem like sufficient punishment. I need someone to mock me, to tell me exactly what kind of person I am.

I text him and, while I wait for a reply, go downstairs to make myself a cappuccino.

Like every morning, Dolores has set a place for me at the breakfast table. The sight of the plate, a napkin on top of it, folded just so, and the cutlery on the side, a little spoon above, just floors me. Because it's a sign of Dolores' affection for me. Her love. And I've gone and squandered it.

# CHAPTER NINETEEN

● ● ● ● ● ● ● ● ● ● ● ● ● ● ● ● ● ○

Jeremy arrives at the house around ten. By then I've paced all about the place, through every room—except for Ian's old bedroom. I've done the dishes. I've removed all my remaining clothing from Dolores' bedroom and put the sheets in the washing machine.

Dolores has a cleaner who comes in every afternoon. She won't have a lot to do today. I wonder what she must think of this. She must know I've been sleeping in Dolores' room. I never had any reason to hide it before.

"Hey, Soph." Jeremy gives me a long, un-Jeremy-like hug—he's usually more the air-kissing type. "How are you?" He smiles sheepishly, as though he's the one who did something so wrong he can't even put it into words. "God, I love this place." He heads further into the house, admiring it all over again. "If I were you, I wouldn't want to leave either."

After I've made us both a cappuccino—my third of the day already—we sit on the living room couch and I suddenly consider how easy it is for me to have a friend over, how this house has become my home.

"Thanks for coming all the way to the Gold Coast."

"You know I love coming here. Once my party days are over, I plan to retire here. Though, of course, prices are through the roof now."

I expel a big sigh, bite my bottom lip.

"What is it?" he asks.

As tears of pure agony pearl in the corner of my eyes, I blurt out, "I slept with her, Jeremy. I slept with Dolores." I let my head fall into my cupped hands, unable to face even my very best friend.

I hear Jeremy put his coffee cup onto the table. I can't look at him, but was that a gasp?

"Damn, girl," Jeremy says. "I truly never thought you had it in you."

I look up into Jeremy's astounded face. "What's that supposed to mean?"

"You've been sleeping in her bed for months. A man's mind can't help but go there from time to time. I just never had you pegged for the type. Not that I consider you a prude, but you are very proper and all of that. Very traditional. A little uptight sometimes."

"What are you talking about?" This is not how I had expected this conversation to go. "She's Ian's mother, for crying out loud."

Jeremy leans back in the couch. "How much do you hate yourself right now?"

I shake my head. "I can't even begin to tell you."

"I know you, Soph. I know you never set out to seduce your mother-in-law. I know you were wrapped in this bubble of coziness and comfort and trying to make sense of it all together. Things happen, that's all. You can't beat yourself up over this. You can't take any more beatings. Be kind to yourself."

"I don't think you're fully getting this. *I* started it. *I* kissed her. I kissed her for the first time yesterday morning and then I kissed her again last night. I kissed her and... and we had sex, Jeremy. I wanted her so badly, because it made me feel so good, but at what cost?"

"Exactly," Jeremy says. "At what cost?"

"I'm going to have to move out of here. Start dealing with stuff I've been avoiding. I guess it's about time, anyway."

"Do you want my opinion or do you just want to rant?"

"I need someone to tell me in no uncertain terms what

a fool I have been because I know Dolores won't have it in her to do so."

"First, take a deep breath. Second, you're always welcome at my place. But, and this is the point I actually want to make, I don't think you should move out of here at all. You love it here. And I get it. I really do. I fully understand the comfort you and Dolores find with each other, and if that comfort has now taken the shape of sleeping together, really sleeping together, then I really don't see anything wrong with that. Furthermore, Dolores would never call you a fool. She was there as well. As far as I know, and from what you're telling me, you were two consenting adults."

"You're missing the point entirely. She's his mother. It's so wrong. I can't think of anything more wrong."

"Really? How about Ian dying just before his thirty-sixth birthday. *That* is wrong in all sorts of ways. You dealing with it however you see fit is only normal."

That gives me pause. "I just… don't want to lose her."

"You want to go back to how it was before she licked your pussy?"

"Oh Christ." I actually manage to utter a little groan of a laugh. "Must you really be so crass? Besides, she didn't *lick my pussy*."

"Oh. I thought that was what you lesbians did primarily. Or is it scissoring?"

"You are such an inappropriate asshole." I can't help but snigger. Because this is what Jeremy does best. Remove the tension from a conversation by making stupid, tasteless jokes. It's what makes his podcast so popular, this total irreverence he has for decorum and boundaries. It's also one of the prime reasons I love him so dearly. It's why I chose to stay with him after Ian's death.

"So, did you lick *her* pussy?" His smile goes up to full beam.

"No, Christ. Do you want all the details?"

"Of course I do, darling. Isn't that why you called me over here?"

"I'll tell you one thing. It was much more satisfying than I ever thought it would be. It kind of blew my mind." Only then do I allow actual memories of pleasure to enter my head again. Maybe I would be able to deal with it better if I hadn't enjoyed it so much.

"Another reason to not beat yourself up about it, Soph. Life is short and it can be really shitty at times. Get your pleasure where you can."

"I guess I was hoping you would judge me more."

"I'm your friend. I only want what's best for you. I've seen you suffer for the past couple of months. While it was great to see you at the party on Saturday, it's even better to see you now. To actually see you smile. To sit next to you after you've truly enjoyed something. Though, and let this be noted for the record, I understand your trepidation. Of course, I do. But it's not up to me to give you a hard time about that. I think you're doing a pretty good job of that yourself."

"I kind of blew Dolores off this morning. I was going to go to the gallery with her."

"You can still go. You texted me at an ungodly hour. You have all day."

"But it's so awkward. Where do we even go from here? I can't possibly get into bed with her again tonight. That's simply not an option. Even though it was the one thing that gave me the most comfort. The proximity of another human being. Not just anyone, but Dolores with all her unconditional love for me."

"Well, unless you plan on becoming a lesbo—and you can skip the U-Haul phase, by the way—you can't sleep in her bed forever."

I nod. "I just can't imagine not sleeping there, either. I guess it's back to Ambien for me."

The sound of someone unlocking the front door

startles us both. At first I think it's Theresa arriving early, but then I remember Dolores' promise to come home for lunch, though it's very early for that.

"Oh, hi, Jeremy," she says casually upon entering the living room.

"Good day to you, Dolores." He gets up to kiss her on the cheek, not leaving any air between his lips and her skin.

This puts an abrupt end to the conversation Jeremy and I were having.

"I have to get going. I have a meeting with Jackie O. in exactly twenty-five minutes," he says.

I'm sure it's not true, that he's just making up an excuse to get out of the house and away from the tension that appeared after Dolores walked in.

"Bye, Soph." He opens his arms wide for a hug and when I step into his embrace, he whispers in my ear, "Please be kind to yourself."

# CHAPTER TWENTY

● ● ● ● ● ● ● ● ● ● ● ● ● ● ● ● ● ● ●

"I came home early. I need to be back at the gallery by one thirty," Dolores says after Jeremy has left. "Shall I make us an omelet?"

"Why don't *I* make us an omelet? You sit down for a bit. Relax." I scoot into the kitchen, quickly realizing that anything resembling an omelet I might produce will be vastly inferior to what Dolores could whip up in five minutes. I look around for a pan. Despite having stayed here for more than two months, I'm not very up to speed on the whereabouts of cooking utensils.

"Sophie," Dolores says, leaning a hip against the kitchen counter. "I came home to talk to you. I'm sorry we didn't have time this morning. Leave the eggs for a minute. I'm not very hungry anyway."

Overcome by a fresh bout of nerves, I blurt out, "I told Jeremy. I had to tell someone. I'm sorry."

"It's okay. Just calm down so we can have an actual conversation about this." Her eyes are pleading. This must be messing with her head as well.

I pull back a chair, its feet scraping noisily over the kitchen floor. "I don't know what there is to talk about. It was a mistake. A moment of weakness. It will never happen again."

Dolores sits next to me. "You're making it sound like you were the only one who had a part in what happened," she says. "I was there too. What happened did so because it's what we both wanted. Because it was that kind of moment. Because we had a lovely evening together—as lovely as we can have. It made me feel good, Sophie. It made me feel human. I'm sorry that you're freaking out about it, but I'm not sorry that it happened."

"But... it's not right." Jeremy's words from before echo in my mind. So many things are not right.

"Who is here to tell us what's right or not? Think about it. The only judge of this is the two of us."

"You may not have any moral objections, but I certainly do." How different it is to have this conversation with Dolores. Earlier, with Jeremy, I craved being judged, being told off, being made to feel as though I committed the worst kind of sin.

Sitting next to Dolores changes everything. Her eyes rest on me, eyes that have found a sparkle again. Her calm voice full of conviction. The memory of her hands and how, for a few minutes, they took away the worst of my pain.

Because I was the one who started it. There are no two ways about it. Now that a few hours have passed since I woke to the evidence of my shocking behavior, and Jeremy has told me not to be too hard on myself, and Dolores sits next to me with that halo of limitless kindness emanating from her, things are different once again. Right now, I can suddenly understand why I did what I did. Why my moral compass didn't stop me when it had the chance. My world is made up out of Dolores. Now that Ian is gone, it's all her. She is beautiful, and eloquent, and attentive, and her kindness knows no boundaries. I'm falling for her. This is love. Not the kind that takes over your mind when you first meet someone and fall head over heels in love. Not the kind that grows between two people when friendship is no longer enough. But the kind of love that is born from acute need, from kinship, from a pain so ruthless it leaves nothing in its wake.

"I know the reason we're so close is only because I'm Ian's mother. It's what brought us together. But there's more between us now. I think we both know that."

"Do you, er, have feelings for me?" My heart slams against my ribcage.

"Of course I have feelings for you. But that's not even the point." She turns to me fully, grabs my hand. My heart starts hammering more feverishly. "I don't want you to feel bad about this. Because if that's all it does then it's indeed not right."

"I have so many things running through my mind."

"I understand that." Dolores curls her fingers around my wrist. "But please bear in mind that nobody got harmed by our actions and, by God, we are still alive, Sophie. My son is dead, but we are alive. It was so good to be reminded of that. I guess that's what it meant to me. It reassured me that I had other emotions inside of me than infinite sadness and sickening grief. What we did made me feel alive. And I know that no one else could have given me that feeling, because of who we are to one another."

"What are you really saying?" I feel my cheeks flush and I can't help myself. I put a hand on Dolores' and move closer. "That you want to feel like that again?"

"Do *you?*" Dolores' lips are less than an inch from mine. I can smell coffee on her breath. Her perfume drifts up into my nose. I can almost feel the heat of her skin.

I nod but don't inch closer. I need her to come to me, to take that final step, however small.

"I need to be one hundred percent sure this is what *you* want. That you're not about to kiss me just to please me or anything silly like that."

"I want you," I say, surprising myself. But I do. If this is what being kind to myself translates into, then so be it. If we're discussing this in broad daylight and have resorted to kissing at the kitchen table, then so be it. It's me and Dolores against all the other things. United, we can beat this pain. We can find a way to get over this loss, to climb out of this well of sorrow. I know I can't do it alone. That's why, again, in the end, it's me leaning into her, bridging the gap between our mouths. It's me who kisses her.

There's nothing tentative about it when our lips lock. The intention behind it is clear from the get-go. I want Dolores to fuck me again, to fuck my pain away, to give me something of herself, of her strong, courageous spirit.

I clasp my hands behind her neck. Blood travels through my arteries at high speed, pumping, making my skin pulse. To hell with everything else. If this is at all wrong, it wouldn't feel so damn good.

Then Dolores' phone starts ringing. She flinches for a split second—all phone calls will do that to us for the foreseeable future—but then ignores it. The caller is insistent and it rings again and our kiss loses steam, until Dolores pulls away, making an apologetic face. "I'm sorry," she says. "It's probably James. I need to take this."

This gives me time to consider how I went from feeling so guilty to so turned on in a matter of minutes. I only have to look at Dolores for a split second to know. It's her. At first glance, this may be all about grief processing in uncommon ways, but this would never have happened—wouldn't be about to happen again—if Dolores wasn't the magnificent woman that she is. I'm so enthralled with her; I can't find fault with her. But this is not a real life romance. This is her and me hidden away in her house, kissing, giving pleasure, pretending the outside world doesn't exist because, in it, we don't exist. That's probably why, subconsciously, I wanted Jeremy to come here. I needed to tell him in this house and nowhere else.

"I'll be there in fifteen minutes." Dolores hangs up. "I'm really sorry, but I need to head back." She pauses, fixing her gaze on me. "Why don't you come with me? You haven't been to the gallery in ages. You know how much James adores you."

I chuckle. "I don't know what it is with me and gay men. I adore them right back."

"Will you come?" From her imploring glance, I

conclude it would mean a lot to Dolores if I accompanied her.

"I will."

"Good." She gets up and reapplies her lipstick in the reflection of the oven window. "Let's go."

\* \* \*

I haven't seen James, or any of Dolores' employees, since the funeral. Ian made a point of going to every single one of his mother's galleries' opening *and* closing nights, which made him very chummy with the people who work there.

"Sophie, come here." James takes me in his arms. "How have you been holding up?" I have no choice but to push my cheek against his hard chest. It feels so foreign after having rested my head on Dolores' soft bosom for the past weeks. "We should really do something together soon. If you're up to it, of course." James babbles a mile a minute, not to hide his discomfort, but because that's just how he always talks. He has the energy of five people compressed into one.

I make the rounds of the rest of the people I know. I'm hugged so many times, it feels as though the impression of Dolores on my skin is being erased, and I want to pull her into her office at the back of the gallery and have her throw her arms around me, have it just be us again—no other human contact required.

"How about I put you to work?" James asks. "Or I can fix you a Bloody Mary, if you'd rather just drink." He gives me a big fat wink.

"I don't think the boss would approve of drinking this early, but I may take you up on that later." I glance at Dolores, who is trying to explain to the artist she's exhibiting why what he thinks of as his pride-and-joy piece should not be the last in sequence. While I look at her, I feel a pang of hunger flit through me. Not for food. For her.

I remember when Ian and I used to come to shows, how proud he always was of his mom, and how she, too, beamed with pride and accomplishment and pure joy, because this is what she loves to do most in the world. No matter how crowded it got, I'd always notice Dolores, because her sheer exuberance made her stand out. Her flair and her ability to turn small talk into a semi-meaningful conversation about art. The way she put nervous artists at ease. I realize I've admired Dolores for a long time. I should be honored to find myself in her bed every night. Not just because of the person she has always been, the mother to Ian and the patroness to the arts in Chicago, but how, after Ian's death, she inhaled deeply, and dared to face the world. I'm astonished by her bravery, by her ability to work through the pain, to occupy her mind with other matters instead of letting the loss consume her—the way I've been doing.

James has me putting explanatory notes of the artworks in frames that will later be hung on the walls, and pretty soon I'm caught up in the buzz of the place, in the hum of activity. There's drilling going on and lots of loud talk and people milling about and in between it all there's Dolores, striding through the gallery as a beacon of calm, as a point of reference for everyone, not least of all me.

James basically makes me his bitch for the rest of the afternoon, making me color code the guest list in an excel sheet, double check caterer orders, all sorts of mindless tasks that nevertheless succeed in occupying my mind in a way that it doesn't drift to the inevitable every other minute, but instead, offers me a glimpse of a life beyond. A life after. Because, as trite as the cliché is, life does go on. The easiest way to tell is by looking at Dolores. How she has willed it to go on for her, despite losing Ian now, and eight years ago when she lost Angela, of whom a gorgeous picture adorns a wall in her office.

After the work for the day has been done—the opening is on Thursday, but the bulk of the artworks are already fastened in place—James orders take-out and we all sit haphazardly in the gallery's tiny kitchen, eating from containers and recounting trivial stories of the day.

I am grabbed by the easy laughter between the people I'm with, by their banter, their camaraderie. I've worked alone in my home office since I graduated. Always making sure I'm not a slave to corporate interests. Perhaps I tried too hard not to be like my mother, instead of getting close to colleagues and going to after-work drinks. By the time everyone is ready to call it a night and head home, I'm convinced that my future doesn't lie with novel writing in a solitary room. I need people around me. Things are different now that I'm alone.

# CHAPTER TWENTY-ONE

●●●●●●●●●●●●●●●●●●●

When we get home, Dolores, uncharacteristically, slips out of her shoes and crashes down on the couch, much as Ian did after a long day at work.

"My feet are killing me," she says. "Haven't had a hectic day like this in a while." She looks at me. "Thanks for coming. I appreciate your help."

I settle next to Dolores' feet and put them in my lap. "You do know I didn't actually do anything. James just gave me some occupational therapy." I rub my thumb over the sole of her foot.

"That feels good." Dolores lets her head fall back in, what I imagine, might be the same kind of pose as if I did to her what she did to me last night.

I intensify my efforts, putting all I have into this impromptu foot massage because, from somewhere deep inside of me a little voice rises, saying that, despite what Dolores might claim, I do owe her. Not just for the orgasm —it's not that plainly tit for tat. But for everything she has done for me. Taken me in. Urged me to go to work with her today. Spoke so kindly to me this afternoon. Big things and small things alike. Again, as I go to work on her big toe, I'm struck by the thought that I'm falling for her, in my own twisted little way. And I want her, oh, I do. I decidedly do not want to end up in the guest bedroom tonight, not that I think there's a lot of chance of that happening.

"I can't thank you enough for that," Dolores groans when I let go of her feet.

"Please, Dolores. A little foot massage is nothing

compared to everything you've done for me."

"Don't underestimate yourself. Don't underestimate the simple power of just you being here with me. Of your willingness to come here in the first place." She sits up a little, bending her legs and pulling them into her chest. "After Angela died, Ian came to stay with me and having him here meant so much. To both of us. Now that he's dead, now that they've both gone." Her voice fractures a little. "I thank whatever lucky stars I have left that you're here. I frankly don't know what I'd do without you."

"You'd soldier on," I say. "The way you did today. I watched you and I was amazed by your strength."

"Don't be fooled by my capacity to put on a show. It's not strength, it's pure need. I'd wither away if I stayed home and did nothing all day."

"It's inspiring." Already missing her touch, I shuffle a little closer, hooking an arm behind her legs. "To me. And I need all the inspiration I can get."

"You're welcome to join me at the gallery any time. It's going to be a busy week. And…" Her voice breaks a little more. "It'll be the first opening night Ian doesn't attend."

"I'll be there. I know I can't be there for the both of us, or make up for his absence, but I'll be there."

"Have you thought about next Saturday?" She looks at me from under her lashes and I see a tear glisten in her eye.

"He would have been thirty-six." Dolores' tears are contagious.

"I've been thinking that maybe we should do something. Throw a party of some sort to celebrate the life he did have. Invite all his friends. I think he would have liked that."

"Are you up for that?" I ask, tears raining down my cheeks.

"Ian and I had a party on Angela's first birthday after her death. She would have been fifty-eight. Her life was surely way too short, but she lived, you know? She sucked the marrow right out of life. We wanted to celebrate that instead of sitting around all day, moping, not knowing what to do with our grief. It was a memorable day and isn't that what we want? To remember our loved ones appropriately?"

I met Ian not long before his mother would have turned sixty. Instead of going to the cemetery, we went to the zoo, because Angela loved going to the zoo so much.

"He did always love a good party," I say.

"Are you comfortable with having one?" Dolores grabs my hand. "We don't have to decide tonight."

I nod while intertwining my fingers with hers—as our lives have become. "It wouldn't just be in Ian's honor. It would be good for me. Perhaps *enjoy* is the wrong word, but that party at Jeremy's last Saturday really helped me. It's good to share and to tell stories, even though I've heard them all a thousand times before. It's good for our friends as well."

"I think I would enjoy having them over."

"I'll take care of it. It'll keep me occupied for a bit. Just let me know who you want to invite that I don't know."

"That's very gracious of you."

"Some of your grace must be rubbing off on me." I smile at Dolores. Her cheeks still glisten with tears.

"You know one twisted thing I'm grateful for? I'm not saying that I wouldn't have wanted her by my side for this, but I'm glad Angela never had to deal with the death of her only child. She was a strong woman, but it would have crushed her. Ian was so very important to her. His happiness was always on her mind. She was devastated when Mandy dumped him. She was already very weak when it happened and Ian and I talked about not telling Angela, but that was not the kind of relationship they had. They were so close and they always wanted nothing but the truth, no matter how difficult, when it concerned each other."

"You would have been strong for her, the way you are for me," I mumble.

Dolores gives me a glance that lingers. "The past

couple of years, Ian was always on my case about me putting myself out there more, about being more willing to meet someone else, but I was never interested enough to actively pursue it. If someone had come my way, I would have considered it, but I never met anyone who could fill Angela's shoes. Which is perhaps my bad, because that's really not the right way to go about it. I shouldn't have been looking out for a second Angela, because such a person doesn't exist." She brings our joined hands from beneath her bent legs and brings them to her face, then plants a kiss on one of my knuckles. "And look at me now. I guess I only realized after Ian's death that being alone can be so very excruciating." She kisses my hand again. "Not that I would want to imply that this is anything more than it is, but I have to admit that I'm glad you didn't pack your bags and move out today."

"I was freaking out this morning. I couldn't believe what happened when I first opened my eyes."

"If it's any consolation, neither could I." Dolores only removes her lips from my hand to speak. As soon as she's done, she turns my hand around and peppers kisses onto my palm.

"Once I stopped panicking..." Her kisses are having an immediate effect. "I kind of wanted it to happen again."

"Do you think we should finish what we started in the kitchen earlier today?" Dolores' voice is confident again, dripping with seduction.

"Hm," I hum, bring my other hand underneath her legs and pull them down, flattening her on the couch. I slide on top of her, one knee between her legs and the other resting next to her, and say, "I do."

Arrows of lust shoot through me. Or maybe it's not lust; it could be something else, but I have no way of knowing the difference. All I know is that Dolores is so easy to talk to, to confide in, to put my heart on display to, and what I'm about to do—because I want to see her succumb under my touch the way I did under hers—is just a logical consequence of the intimacy that has grown between us. We're together, and maybe not in a traditional sense, but that too can be construed as an honor to Ian's memory, because he hardly came from a traditional family.

I kiss Dolores, again. Kissing her is so different from anyone else I've ever kissed. It's not just the softness, the tenderness that reaches every fiber of my being when our lips meet, it's the inevitability and the sense that, even though it's the complete opposite of what I felt when I woke up this morning, it's right. That there is no other way for us than this one. And it's sensual, and arousing, and gratifying when she hums low in her throat like she is doing now, and I'm so ready to lose myself again. I'm ready for it here and now on her couch.

My pulse picks up speed. I'm intoxicated by the prospect of what I'm about to do. It's all new to me, and so extremely exciting. Plus I'm about to do it to Dolores, whom I adore—whom I love, probably more than any other living person on this earth.

When we break from our kiss, Dolores is flustered. Her hair is a little mussed and her lipstick smudged. "Are you sure?" she asks, as though she can read my intention from my face. Maybe she can. Maybe it's a secret power lesbians have, like a sixth sense.

"Oh yes." I start tugging off my clothes, because this is not going to be a slow process like last night. The entire afternoon I spent at the gallery was basically foreplay. I want Dolores here and now. I want her spread wide for me. I want to dive headfirst into this new adventure that is making my head spin a little and my clit throb a lot.

"Hold on," she says, pushing herself upward before hoisting her blouse over her head.

The way we're approaching things now is a far cry from last night's slow burn. In fact, this is the first time I see Dolores in her bra, though my gaze is not drawn to her torso, but to her face, still majestic with its high cheekbones and crystal blue eyes, but also intense, her stare determined as she throws the piece of garment away from her, discards it like the barrier it has now become. The only thing keeping me from devouring her. Because that's what it feels like. I want to devour her, have her, make her mine in a way that's not even sensible, but pulses through me nonetheless.

She reaches for the button of my jeans next, then tugs them off me unceremoniously. This frenzy is no less sexy than the slow movement of my hand with which I gingerly pulled her tank top away from her belly button last night, but it *is* different. It's more insistent, more brazen in its inevitability and purpose. We are sitting underneath the low but clear light of Dolores' living room lamp. It's not even fully dark yet outside. This is us saying yes to the daytime, to not doing this in the obscure embrace of the night. This is me saying yes to Dolores a thousand times over. It roars through me like a low rumble, a thunder in my flesh, a tension in my muscles.

In no time, we have our clothes off, except for our underwear, and only then do I take a breather to assess the situation. As far as I know, I'm as heterosexual as they come. Unlike Alex, I didn't have the requisite college lesbian experience. If there is a spectrum of sexuality, which I don't doubt but never gave much thought to, I'm in the far corner saying one hundred percent. At least, I was. Because the sight of Dolores, of her pale, fragile skin, of her vulnerability on display, enthralls me. And I can repeat to myself over and over again that this isn't sexual, that it's grief finding a way out through sins of the flesh, or some other therapeutic mumbo jumbo, but it would be a lie. It would be a lie to not recognize this as exactly what it is. This is me, Sophie Winters, being aroused beyond the point of no return by another woman. A woman who is twenty-six years my senior. A woman who floors me by sinking a row of teeth into her bottom lip, by a gentle flick of the wrist toward me, by her desire for me, because it's blazing unmistakably in her eyes now. Is this love? Oh, yes. No doubt about it. Is it forbidden, delicious, unbridled lust? Equally so. I want all of Dolores with all I have left after Ian's death, which might not be much. But I'm still me. I'm still breathing, and right now every single breath stokes the fire in my belly more, because one thing is for absolute certain: I'm about to make love to Dolores.

She sits on the couch, and leans back. When I look at her, it's as though I just know what to do. Granted, it's not rocket science. I'm just following my carnal instinct, which only has one place to lead me: between her legs. I hook my fingertips underneath the waistband of her silk maroon panties, and, in what is the only really calculated gesture up until now, slide them off her in a controlled movement, my thumbs caressing her skin. Dolores takes care of removing her bra and then I must really take pause. It's not a deliberate one, more one born from utter stupefaction, not only at this moment, but at Dolores' willingness to do this, to sit here like this, for me. I have never been religious, not before Ian's death, and certainly not after, but I somehow feel the need to recognize this as a spiritual moment, of mine and Dolores' souls joining forces and, entwined, combusting into unfathomable lust. A desire so big, it pushes everything out of my brain but the singular thought of licking her. Every single thing. Even the one thing that will be a part of me forever. Becoming a not-even-widow at the age of thirty. It's gone. In that moment, I'm not a bereaved woman. Dolores is not my deceased partner's mother. This is us, this spark between us is solely fueled by us, by what's been growing between us, what's been fostered in the messy bed of our grief.

When I lower my head between Dolores' thighs, I'm instantly enveloped by her warmth, her scent, her most intimate aroma. I kiss her inner thighs, tentatively at first, because, underneath all this passion, I do still have my insecurities. I've never done this before. But I'm doing it now. Especially because Dolores brings her hands into my hair, and her touch is so gentle, so nurturing, that I can't stop myself any longer. My lips land on her sex and I kiss my way up and down, slowly at first, still finding my feet, but I soon do, and open my mouth and let my tongue flick out, stroking her clit.

"Oh," she moans, and the intensity of her groan touches me deep inside, makes my own clit pulse, makes me want her fingers inside of me again.

Then I let loose, because I have no expertise in teasing another woman like this. Besides, we're past teasing. I mean business and I'm here, with my head now clasped between Dolores' thighs, to prove it. Her fingers brush against my scalp. She doesn't guide me, only spurs me on, indicates that she's enjoying this—though her moans alone are evidence enough. I let my tongue dance over her clit, burrow between her lips, taste her, drink her in, and all the while an augmenting desire takes hold of me, blistering the surface of my skin, trying to find a way out of me. I channel that desire into the tip of my tongue, focus all of it on Dolores, to whom I want to give this so much, though this doesn't entirely feel like giving. I'm taking from this as much as I'm giving away. With every flick of my tongue, an unknown energy builds in me, swoops through my belly, engorges my clit. When this is over, I'm absolutely certain I won't be as gallant as Dolores was with me last night. I'll need some sort of release. Her fingers inside of me again or, perhaps, her tongue waltzing over my clit like mine is over hers. I suck her clit between my lips, lick it up and down, all around, and imagine arriving at this moment through a different chain of actions and reactions. A calmer, quieter, more deliberate way of making love. Because I'm not making the mistake of labelling this as fucking. Dolores and I, we are making love. It might be frenzied, feverish, with a touch of mania, but this is love. Maybe not romantic love, but right now it all feels the same to me.

"Oh. God." Dolores' moans grow more high-pitched, more out of control. To have this effect on another woman is so intoxicating, the heat inside me starts to boil over. All that was dead and cold inside of me has found a new warmth, a brand new way of coming alive again.

Dolores' hands grip firmly now, locking me, for all intents and purposes, in a prison of her thighs and sex. I keep licking and flicking and sucking, wondering whether this is always all it takes, whether this kind of sapphic love-making usually requires a little more finesse, but then I consider that any form of subtlety would have been wasted on the heated situation in which we found ourselves—and lucky for me that it did. This way, I have time to hone my new-found skill, though skill is probably a big word for it.

"Oh, Sophie," Dolores exclaims and lets go of my head, lets her knees fall wide. Juicy remnants of her climax stick to my chin, and I wipe them off as best I can with the back of my hand, gloating a little on the inside, though trying hard not to show it, because, damn, that was glorious.

"Come here," Dolores says and I climb up to her. "Come here my beautiful, gorgeous darling." She pulls me close and kisses me all over my mouth, my cheeks, my jaw. "That was amazing." Then she bursts out into a little uncharacteristic chuckle. "I have no earthly idea how long it's been since someone last did that to me."

"It's an honor," I joke, though I also recognize the more serious side of this. Only a brief while ago Dolores was telling me how, after Angela, nobody interesting enough crossed her path.

"I have less honorable intentions for you." She topples me onto my back. "First, let's get these off you." Traces of wetness trickle down my thighs as Dolores pulls down my panties. It feels as though every last one of my cells is pulsing, screaming for release. "Now, let's see."

Without the slightest hesitation, Dolores brings her hand between my legs.

"Oh my," she says, a hint of a smile playing on her lips, "something left someone a tad hot and bothered."

I don't care if she teases me. I'm well beyond being teased. Right now, Dolores' finger is enough to shut me up for a good long while, or at least until I come.

"Looks like you're greatly enjoying this red hot affair of ours," she says, while, slowly, so slowly, circling her finger around my clit.

"Oh, please," I beg. "Please. Dolores." Her name comes out as a whimper, a faint cry for help.

"Don't worry, Sophie." She ramps up the pace of her finger. "I've got your back." Her voice is low and gravelly, her eyes, still on me—and I can't look away, not this time— narrow, the blue barely shining through her hooded eyelids. "Come for me," she says then, and I can hardly believe she would say that, as though it's even a question you can ask someone. I can't possibly come just because she asks me to. There's a little more to it than that. "Will you come for me?" she repeats, and the speed at which her finger circles my clit increases. "Will you?" Her voice is a whisper, but a powerful one, because, much to my surprise, it connects with something inside me, the flame that's been roaring in my belly since I started licking her, since she bared every last inch of herself to me.

I'm not sure if it's because she asked me or because I'm so well beyond the point of no return, but the first spasm travels through my muscles. Dolores stops the circles now and flicks the tip of her finger against my clit, over and over again, and it's too much, she's too much; I love her; I need her. I never want to leave her.

I am foolish, silly for even having these thoughts but they pass through my mind nonetheless as I give myself up to her. All of me. Pain and all. What Dolores has done is transformed my pain into joy—and how is that even possible?

# CHAPTER TWENTY-TWO

By the gallery's opening night, Dolores and I have explored each other's bodies every chance we got. I know that, strangely, her left nipple is more sensitive than her right. I've traced the faint birth mark she has on the back of her thigh with my tongue numerous times. I know what she smells like, and notice the difference in the morning and in the evening. As I stand under the bright lights of the gallery, it feels as though all we've been doing is having sex. Not just for the past couple of days, but for months. That's how much she is in my head, how much she is part of me.

I've come to the gallery a couple of times with Dolores and whereas before we started making love like two teenagers who have just discovered the joys of sex, I wouldn't have thought twice about what Dolores' employees might think of me being at the gallery all the time, now I often wonder if they somehow know. James, who spends a lot of hours with Dolores, must know her so well. He must be able to tell that there's something different about her. Or perhaps he just automatically chalks the subtle difference in her complexion up to a new stage of grief. Maybe he thinks the tad more confidence in her gait is just down to time passing.

And tonight, she shines. I feel sorry for the artist her gallery is displaying, with his wooden demeanor and overly visible self-consciousness. He's not meant for the spotlight, I can so easily tell. He prefers making his collages—paint over print—in the solitude of his studio. But he needn't worry, because he has Dolores on his side. For a nice percentage, she'll do the heavy lifting of selling his work for him.

I wander around the crowd, nod back at people politely when they offer one, and catch snippets of Dolores' voice while I wait for Jeremy to arrive. Whenever she speaks, I remember how her voice lowered to a whisper as she demanded that I come. Just watching her move about the place makes my skin tingle again, to the extent that I begin to wonder what the hell is going on with me.

We're well into the twenty-first century, and sexuality is supposed to be fluid; one is supposed to question it from time to time in this post-post-modern age, but I never have and that's what throws me the most. Does sleeping with Dolores make me bisexual? Does it even matter?

"Hey stranger." I hear Jeremy's voice coming from behind me. "You've been M.I.A." His tone is not accusatory, only teasing. "Let me guess—" Luckily, he doesn't finish his sentence. Despite his lack of decorum, Jeremy knows all about time and place. This is not the place for him to say certain things to me.

"I've been busy." I kiss him on each cheek, then inspect his attire. He's dressed in an electric blue suit, white shirt and very yellow slim tie. Vintage Jeremy.

"Oh, I'm sure you have been, darling. How's that novel coming along?" His tone is full of innuendo. "Is it an erotic novel, I wonder? I hear they're going out of fashion so you'd better hurry."

"I don't want to write a novel anymore. I can't bear to sit in a room for hours alone with my thoughts. It would drive me mad. I don't know what I was thinking."

"Jackie O. will be so pleased." He examines me. "You look good, Soph. Better. And, of course, I'll be at the party on Saturday. Am I allowed to call it that?"

"Yes. It's a party to celebrate Ian's life."

"Hello, my dear." June, one of Dolores' closest friends and fellow art aficionado, greets me by putting a hand on my shoulder. I've gotten to know her a little over the years. She and Dolores go way back and I was told they're about the same age, except June seems to look at least ten years older than Dolores. "So good of you to come and support Dolores."

Jeremy and I exchange a quick glance.

"She's been a big support to me," I reply.

June nods thoughtfully and I can't help but wonder if Dolores has told her about us. After all, I've told Jeremy. But he's Jeremy. It seems different, but, of course, it's not. Why would Dolores not need someone to confide in? Maybe I'm wrong to assume things are different at their age. *Their age.* It makes me question again what the hell Dolores and I are doing. I can explain away our motives all I want, but what is the outcome here? The end game? More pain? It's not as if we can possibly ever really be together. Attend an opening night like this as a couple. It's unthinkable.

June gets wrapped up in conversation with someone who's tapped her on the back, which allows me to refocus my attention on Jeremy. I'm so grateful to him for coming. Because this is my first art gallery reception without Ian too. When we used to come here together, he'd be milling about the place, helping his mother to put the artist at ease—he had that way with people—and then, when guests started to leave, and he'd had a little too much champagne, he would whisper in my ear, "What do you think, babe? Should I follow in my mother's footsteps, stop being an architect and join the world of the arts?" It was one of many plans he had. One of the many that he will never get to carry out. Out of nowhere, by the sheer force of that memory, there's the anger again. Isn't it absolutely ludicrous to have a birthday party for someone who's dead? Who will never have another birthday? Instinctively, I try to locate Dolores in the crowd, try to find her gaze for support.

"So what are your new career plans, Soph?" Jeremy's voice cuts through my train of gloomy thoughts just as a waiter passes and offers us a new glass of champagne. We both eagerly accept. I have to keep myself from knocking it back in a few big gulps.

"I'm not sure yet. While I figure it out, I'll just help out here. It's the least I can do for Dolores."

Jeremy looks at me with that semi-condescending stare he's so good at, but doesn't say anything.

"What?" I drink again.

"Sweetie, I know your world has been turned upside down and I get that you're questioning *everything*"—a lot of emphasis there—"but I hope you're not doing any of this because you feel you owe it to Ian's mother."

I open my mouth to protest but he holds up his hand, signaling he's not done yet.

"You're a damn good journalist. They don't make 'em like you anymore. It's like the airiness and swiftness of journalism in this day and age doesn't affect you at all. You're only thirty and you already have such a solid reputation. *The Post* would miss you if you threw in the towel."

Even though I'm flattered by what he just said, I'm too hung up on his first sentence to bask in his kind words. "I don't feel like I owe Dolores." I realize it's a big fat lie as the words cross my lips and it gives me pause. "At least not the way you're insinuating," I correct myself.

"We shouldn't talk about this now." Jeremy's features turn all mushy and apologetic. "Let's have lunch or dinner tomorrow. Whenever suits you. I'll make time. Come to mine. I'll make you eggs benedict on avocado toast." He flutters his lashes.

"You're bribing me with food?"

"Bribing? I'm your best friend and I want to have a conversation with you. That's not a bribe, only a normal request."

"Hi, Jeremy." James joins us.

Jeremy is right. This isn't the right place to have a conversation about any of these things. Besides, I need some time to figure stuff out.

Jeremy and James start talking—James being a total fan boy and Jeremy enjoying every second of it. I focus my attention back on the room while I empty my champagne flute. Dolores is headed in my direction, determination in her tread, nodding at a few people but not stopping to talk to them.

"Want to go into my office for a minute?" she whispers in my ear.

I nod and follow her and as I do, I can almost feel Jeremy's glance burn into my back.

* * *

As soon as we enter Dolores' office she closes the door and locks it. She turns around, her back against the door, and says, "I'm falling apart, Sophie."

I'm shocked but also not, because I know how she feels. I take a step closer and throw my arms around her.

"Everyone either asks me how I'm doing or looks at me with a pity in their glance I just can't bear." Her voice is muffled because her mouth is somewhere in my hair, but I hear her loud and clear. "I feel like it's not about Vasily or his art at all tonight, but it's all about me, and Ian, who, even though he's no longer here, is very present."

I hold her a little closer. "I know."

"It's so hard. I miss him so much and it's just so damn hard." Her muscles stiffen. She takes a deep breath, and another. "It's so unfair," she mumbles as she frees herself from my arms. "I really shouldn't cry." She brings a finger underneath her eye, trying to stop her mascara from running. "It's like it only just now really hit me, on this night that doesn't even have anything to do with him. I thought it would be a breeze, keeping busy, engaging in my usual chit chat, because this is what I'm good at. But with every person's hand I shook or cheek I kissed, the question in my head grew louder: what's the point? What am I even doing here? He was not supposed to go before me, Sophie. I was supposed to be a grandmother to his children. I was supposed to tell him off for sneaking a cigarette once in a while even though his other mother died of lung cancer. I was supposed to look for him tonight, see him peek out of the crowd with his tall body, with that easy smile on his face. He was such a charmer. He loved nights like this."

"I know, Dolores, I know." The words barely make it past the lump in my throat. "But we have no choice. We must plow through. It's the only way. I know it's unfair. Life is unfair, but it's all we have. We owe it to him to live."

Someone knocks gently on the door. "Dolores," James says in a hushed voice, "are you there? Can I come in?"

"Just a minute, James."

I witness how Dolores pulls herself together in front of my eyes. The metamorphosis is astounding. She goes from crumpled mother who lost her son to straight-backed gallery owner in the space of seconds.

"We all fall apart," I say. *It's how we get back up that defines us*, I think but don't say out loud. Because Dolores obviously knows how to put herself back together. I've just witnessed her do it in such an expert fashion it makes me feel like the biggest amateur. Which I am.

She dabs a tissue underneath her eyes, casts a glance at Angela's picture, gives my hand a quick squeeze and opens the door.

I watch her as she walks off with James, as though the past five minutes didn't even happen. I'm the only witness to her moment of weakness. It's what keeps us together.

# CHAPTER TWENTY-THREE

●●●●●●●●●●●●●●●●●●●●●

*Ian,*

*I don't even know how to begin this letter. I can hardly say "Happy Birthday", can I? And then there's that other thing…*

*Let me start by saying that we're having a party in your honor today. You would have been thirty-six. Everyone is coming. Alex and Bart, Sydney and Ethan, Jeremy. Some of Dolores' friends as well, the ones you always charmed with your geeky wit and overly courteous manners. June and Helen, Patsy.*

*But this was not how it was supposed to be. If you were still alive, I know that, as usual, we wouldn't have made any plans, and we'd have probably ended up at your mother's for dinner and a bottle of champagne, but, well, you were supposed to be here for this, Ian. You were not supposed to die. You were not supposed to leave and let us 'celebrate' your birthday without you. And…*

*There's something else. Something has happened, but I feel like when I write it down, it will become more than it is. It will become something official. Something I can't deal with in that capacity. As long as I keep it just in my head, it's not as real as I want it to be. It is real, but also strangely not.*

*Oh fuck, Ian. You're not going to believe this. You may actually want to die, not by accident but by choice, after hearing this. But let me tell you something: the only reason why I ended up in Dolores' bed is because you did die. It's the only reason. I can't seem to stress that enough.*

*We haven't just been sleeping. We've been… I don't know how to call it. Comforting each other in other ways. I don't want to use the f word. It's too crass for the tenderness we have between us. For the love we share. A love born solely from shared love for you.*

*You brought us together, so please don't judge me, wherever you are.*

*Dolores and I have been making love. Christ. It sounds so trite. So wrong, spelled out like that. But I do have feelings for her. I do. I just don't know what they mean exactly. All I know is that being with Dolores makes me feel infinitely better. Sometimes, when I wake up, I smile when I see her. I actually smile when I open my eyes. Isn't that a miracle in itself? I never thought I'd smile again. I never thought I'd feel anything like this again.*

*I probably shouldn't be telling you this. You don't want to hear. But guess what, Ian? You no longer have any say in the matter, in any matter, because you're dead. And what was I supposed to do after that?*

*The thought of another guy simply repels me. That would feel like cheating. Being with Dolores doesn't. Granted, the taboo aspect turns me on. It does. How can it not? But that's not what it's about. Dolores is such a spectacular woman. Sometimes, she lets herself fall apart in my arms, and I always consider her even more spectacular afterwards. She lets go for me, in more ways than one, and I'm honored that she does. We're so close now, she can probably read my thoughts. We can just sit in silence and have the same thoughts running through our heads. It's pretty magical, come to think of it.*

*And yes, Ian, I can hear you think it. Am I a lesbian now? Have I gone gay for your mother? Though, please allow me to point out, which I've been doing to myself a lot, that she's not your biological mother. Not even your stepmother. I know how much it would have hurt you—and Dolores—if I'd said those things while you were alive. But you not being alive is what set this whole thing in motion in the first place. And yes, I use it as an excuse. Every single time. Every single day.*

*You're dead and I'm sleeping with your mother. How fucked up is that? It actually makes me chuckle as I write this. It's ridiculous. Maybe I should do some research on the subject. There must be some literature on this, some study conducted by an obscure university. And, oh my god, Ian, imagine my mother's face if she were to find out. Imagine the shock. No boardroom experience can prepare you for your* daughter sleeping with her (non-biological!) mother-in-law.

But you have to understand. As perverted or depraved or sick as this may be, I need to get my comfort where I can now. My smile in the morning, that miracle, that little glimmer of being glad I'm alive because I'm waking up next to her, even if it lasts only a split second, it's all I have. It's what keeps me going. It's what stops me wishing I was buried with you. Dolores is my lifeline. Nobody may ever understand, but we do.

I may never read this letter again, but there... Now you know. The ink has dried on the page.

This is what your dying has done to me.

Fuck, I love you. I miss you. Our friends will be here soon. I'm supposed to get all dolled up for this party. I went back to the apartment—into our bedroom—especially to get that teal dress you liked so much on me. And for what? Are you looking down on me from your comfortable spot in heaven? I sometimes wish I was gullible enough to be religious, but I'm not. Not one little bit. My loss, really.

So much is my loss these days.

I miss you.

Sophie

# CHAPTER TWENTY-FOUR

●●●●●●●●●●●●●●●●●●●●●

At the party, I just drink. I drink and I feel like a cliché—except when I look at Dolores. Then I feel like anything but.

Everyone we invited has come, because how can you possibly turn down an invitation for a dead man's birthday? It's not an option. All selfishness, all other plans, are trumped by death.

As I sit in a chair and drink more, totally neglecting my duties as hostess—Dolores and Jeremy are picking up the slack—I also feel mightily sorry for myself. I shouldn't have written that letter to Ian just before people started arriving. What was supposed to be an activity that brought me some sort of solace, some closure, has begun to make me feel like a freak. A freak wallowing in self-pity. The absolute opposite of what Ian would want me to be.

Everyone keeps repeating what a great guy he was. If I have to hear that particular phrase one more time, I'm not sure what I will do. Everything is just so fucked. As if I actually want to snuggle up to Dolores each and every night. No. What I want is for Ian to have left the apartment one minute later that morning, for him to have taken an alternative route, for me to have kissed him profusely before he left, making him late, making him miss the reversing truck. Keeping him alive.

*I could have kept him alive.*

Instead, I'm sitting here, surrounded by people but feeling more alone than ever. Dolores is chatting with her friends. She must have quite a few things to say to them, the way she's gesticulating. Perhaps she's just happy to have a conversation with people her age for a change.

"Come on, you." Jeremy tugs at my elbow. "Mingle. Turn that frown upside down. You can't just sit here with that scowl on your face all afternoon."

"Excuse me?" I shake him off me.

"Sweetie, I know exactly what's going on in that head of yours. And while I understand, you invited all these people here. They came here for you—"

"They came for Ian's irrelevant birthday," I protest.

"No, Soph. They came for you. Can't you see that?" He grabs me by the arm again, gentle but insistent. "I came for you."

"I just... want to talk about something else than what a wonderful, lovely guy Ian was. Just for five minutes," I whisper. "Does that make me a horrible person?"

"No, darling that makes you human. Come on, Bo and Cindy have been asking about you, but have been too timid to approach you. Anyone would be with the way you're sitting here. You have so much in common with them now. Maybe you can ask for some tips."

"Don't push it, Jeremy."

"Apologies, but I'm pushing *you*. You need it."

"Then pour me another drink first."

Jeremy shrugs, grabs a bottle of red wine from the table and refills my glass.

I follow his advice—or command, more like—and mix with the small crowd. There are about twenty people in Dolores' house. Michael, Ian's boss, is here. And Tommy. There's no one here who didn't love him to bits, yet they all get to go home after this *party*, relieved that that ordeal has passed, and get on with their lives. Whereas me, I'll be climbing into Dolores' bed again, trying to forget, trying to forgive myself for not pushing him more to wear a helmet when he rode his bike. "Nobody wears a helmet in Chicago, babe," Ian would say. "This isn't Southern California."

"Hey." Dolores suddenly stands beside me and puts her

arm on my shoulder. "Are you okay?" I can't help it. I flinch a little at her touch. Fearing that my friends will somehow be able to read from my face what we've been doing.

"I'm drunk and I think this party was a bad idea," I mumble, no longer able to keep up appearances in front of Dolores. Having had a dozen orgasms at someone's fingers will do that to you.

"Come on." She places a hand on the small of my back. "Let's get you some coffee." She coaxes me toward the kitchen and closes the door behind us. She sits me down on a chair and pours me a steaming cup.

"The last party I was at, it was different, you know?" I slur my words.

"Drink this." Dolores crouches next to me, her hand on my thigh. "Do you want to go upstairs for a bit? People will understand."

"They will understand what? That we go upstairs together?" The amount of pure rage I'm feeling toward everything and everyone is new. "That we sleep together?"

"Sophie, please." Dolores' nails dig through the flimsy fabric of my dress.

"Why don't we just go into the pantry and fuck while all our friends are out there?" I wave my hand toward the door and knock over a glass of water in the process.

"Please calm down." Dolores pushes herself up and picks up the glass I knocked over. The water I spilled drips onto the kitchen floor.

"I'm sorry." I bury my head in my hands. "My turn for a party breakdown," I mutter into my hands. All the energy I had left, escapes me. I feel as empty as I've ever done. What was supposed to be a celebration of Ian's life has just become a massive reminder of his death, more so than on any regular day. "I'm in a funny mood today," I say when I look back up.

A tear runs down Dolores' cheek.

"It's okay. Come here." She pulls me out of the chair

and wraps her arms around me. "It's okay." With Dolores' hands in my hair and her breath on my neck, and her love and support on display, I can't keep it dry. I cry on her shoulder, wishing I could just disappear, like Ian did, leaving everyone to sort out their subsequent misery without me.

"I know very well it was a stupid accident, but sometimes it just feels like he deserted me. And fuck if I know how to deal with all this… shit." I don't care that I'm swearing in front of Dolores. "Sometimes, I just think he's such an asshole for dying like that. So in vain. So uselessly. Nothing good will ever come of his death. All there is, is pain and grief and loss and endless days of agony and drinking too much and missing him, while the world just keeps on turning. I bet he's been replaced at work. I bet there's nothing where he died to show that anyone lost their life at that spot. The paramedics who were first on the scene have responded to a hundred more calls since then. The bloody truck driver is probably driving along happily, feeling lucky because the police didn't find fault with him. Well, I do. I find him guilty, because the simple fact is that if he hadn't been backing up his truck, Ian would still be alive. He would be celebrating his birthday today. We'd be singing 'Happy Birthday' to him, out of tune, and he would have that goofy grin on his face, and kiss you on the cheek and me on the lips and thank us for our performance, and we would all be so very, stupidly, recklessly happy, not knowing that it can all just end in a split second."

"Oh, Sophie." Dolores kisses me on the cheek first, then she cups my jaw with her hands, and kisses me full on the lips. In her kitchen. While, behind the door, twenty of the people we know best are drinking and chatting and reminiscing.

When she does it again, her lips lingering this time, I'm the one—me, the woman who just drunkenly knocked over a glass of water and yelled at her—who suggests she stop what she's doing.

"Let's go into the pantry," she says. Her eyes are intense.

"What?" I figure I must be too tipsy to have heard her correctly.

"I need you," Dolores says, and takes me by the hand. "Come."

I let myself be dragged into the pantry. When Dolores closes the door behind us, it's pitch black inside. She doesn't switch on the light. Instead, she locks her lips on mine, her hands already traveling underneath my dress.

"Dolores, come on. Are you sure about this?" I try, but hell, I need this too. I need this to snap me out of my funk, out of my stupor of unflattering self-pity. I need Dolores to bring me back to myself again, at least to the version of me who can face her friends in the living room, and toast her dead boyfriend's birthday.

"I am if you are," Dolores says in between moans. She's clearly not waiting for my reply. Her hands have reached my belly already. My dress is pulled all the way over my behind. "I want you," she says, as though she hasn't made that loud and clear yet.

And I want her, too. I need her *and* I want her because, thus far, what we're about to do, is the only thing that cuts through the pain. Alcohol makes me too maudlin. Talking to my friends makes me miss Ian so much more than when I'm alone. Only this, being here with Dolores, brings relief.

So I let her slip her fingers inside my panties while her lips kiss my mouth, my cheeks, my neck. I let Dolores find her own comfort, with me. Because like this, she's not alone and I'm not alone. We are us. Together we can take more.

When two of her fingers delve deep inside of me, and I have one hand in her short blonde hair, the other disappearing into Dolores' panties, I know it's not this physical act that will soothe the worst of my pain. It's not the orgasm, nor how, no matter how deliciously, Dolores already knows how to expertly make me approach it in no time—so much has changed since Ian died. It's how she'll look at me afterwards, how she'll wrap her arms around me, and, her voice all low and tender, she will say a few vapid words that will hold so much meaning nonetheless, just because she said them to me after the fact, and they will connect us so invisibly but indisputably.

When we're done fumbling, our climaxes quick but satisfying in that frenetic, I-must-have-you-now manner, Dolores stands in front of me, her hand in mine. "I don't even care what anyone thinks, Sophie," she says. "Why would I? How could anyone's judgement of me make me feel any worse than how I feel already?"

That sums it up so well.

We are two women with absolutely nothing to lose.

\* \* \*

"Have you lost your mind completely?" Jeremy hisses after Dolores and I have made it back to the living room.

"I was about to, until Dolores set me straight," I reply, not caring how that makes me sound.

"Straight? Funny choice of word." He bumps his shoulder into mine. "Sometimes I wish I didn't know. Why can't I ever be the innocent one?" He actually draws his lips onto a pout.

"Because you're Jeremy Rath. You lost your innocence the day you learned how to speak."

"Wow, it's good to have you back, Soph. That rumble in the kitchen must have done you a world of good."

I square my shoulders and look at him. "Do I need to give a speech?"

"Only if you've sobered up enough." He quirks up his eyebrows. One always goes higher than the other.

"Dolores poured me some strong coffee."

"I'm sure she did, darling." He huffs out a chuckle. "You should do what you want. If you don't feel like it, then don't do it. It's not expected of you. If it will make you feel better, then by all means…"

"Have I thanked you enough for your unwavering support?" I look Jeremy straight in the eyes.

"The only gratitude I want is to see you smile again."

"Christ, when even the notorious Jeremy Rath becomes corny, there's no hope left."

Jeremy's face breaks out into a smile. He leans into me and whispers, "If this is the effect Dolores has on you, then long may it continue."

I play-punch him in the arm. I guess it's as close to his blessing Dolores and I will ever get.

Then I take a deep breath, clear my throat and call the room to attention. At the funeral I was unable to speak, let alone deliver a speech. It has been almost three months since Ian died. I have found some of my voice again and I want to say a couple of things about him to these people he loved.

After having thanked them all for coming and directing my glance firmly above the small crowd's heads, I fix it on Dolores for moral support.

"I'm sure Ian would have liked me to crack a few jokes, but I can't remember any, even though he told me many. He made them up on his way to and from work. That's why he loved riding his bike so much. It cleared his head. Gave him time to think about non-important things like silly jokes. It was his me-time." I pause. I always liked that he rode a bike. I teased him about it, saying he was such a hippie. It never for one second occurred to me that it would kill him some day. I wisely leave the too grim thoughts out of my speech.

"In lieu of telling a joke, let's all raise our glass to Ian. We all know he liked a drink even more than a bad joke." Dolores smiles at me from the other side of the room. I hold up my glass. "To Ian, that handsome architect who rode his bicycle everywhere. We'll never forget him." Of course, then, I well up. Maybe I should have said more, but the more I say about him, the more his absence stings.

Everyone raises their glass and a cacophony of "To Ian" fills the room. And it's only then that I realize that this *was* a good idea. It's cathartic to simply say his name in this group of people, to feel the love for him reverberate through the room.

Dolores is talking to Alex while she dabs a tear from her eye. Most people are sniffling, including Ian's boss. I still think it's all grotesquely unfair and unbearable and too damn hard most days, but I also know that there's only one thing that will get me through this and it's all the love that is trapped in this room.

# CHAPTER TWENTY-FIVE

●●●●●●●●●●●●●●●●●●●●●

Two weeks after Ian's birthday, I meet Jeremy at his apartment. He has cooked for me and the seared tuna he serves is delicious. When we've reached the digestif stage of the meal, he pours me a large brandy, and says, "I think it's time for me to play devil's advocate."

Instantly, I know what he's getting at. We've avoided the subject of Dolores all night. It was bound to come up.

"Have you thought about the future?" he asks. "How long has this been going on?"

"About a month, so not long enough for you to worry about."

"But you must talk, Soph. Do you ever talk about what you want in the long run? Are you moving in permanently?"

"Sometimes," and I know this is two bottles of wine and the few sips of brandy talking more than anything else, but I want to say it anyway, "I do sincerely wonder whether Dolores and I have a future."

Jeremy starts fidgeting with a napkin. "You do?"

"In an ideal world... I don't know." I truly don't know. I might have wondered, or perhaps fantasized is a better word for it, but I've yet to reach any conclusions.

"What would happen in an ideal world?" Jeremy insists.

He has me averting my glance. I know how ridiculous this sounds. I could never say this to anyone else. I inspect the color of my beverage intently while I say, "In an ideal world, I could see us together."

"Really?" Jeremy seems genuinely flabbergasted. "How?"

"How? I don't know how. All I know is that I care about Dolores so, so much. I love her. I can honestly say that with my hand on my heart. I love her, I do. What I have with her far exceeds any expectation I might have had about someday being with someone again. I know it's complicated, but that's why I prefaced it with *in an ideal world*."

"I get all that, but you must realize this is—and, oh my, how it pains me to have to utter these words—a *phase* you're going through. Surely, what you feel for Dolores is not romance."

"Then what is it?" A peculiar calm descends on me now. I had expected to feel more put on the spot.

"Do you really want me to spell it out?" Jeremy twirls his brandy glass between his fingers.

"No need. I know what *you* think it is. You think it's just my grief talking and my mind playing this trick on me because of it, and I don't expect you to understand or believe me, but to me, it's much more than that."

Jeremy sighs. "So you're going to live happily ever after?"

I shake my head. "Of course not, but…" I hold up my hand and start counting down on my fingers. "One: the sex we have is nothing short of spectacular, which baffles me completely, but it's how it is. Two: have you ever met anyone nicer, with more pure goodness in their heart than Dolores? I haven't. Three: she makes me feel like there's hope, and that's probably what's most important. She makes me feel like there's more than that pit of despair I fell into after Ian's death."

"Could it be that you're idealizing her just a little?" Jeremy counters.

"Maybe, but I've been spending *all* of my time with her and I've gotten to know her pretty well, or at least this post-death-of-her-son version of her, and I just—plain and simple—really like her."

"Am I allowed to give you my own countdown of

counter arguments?"

"Sure." I look at Jeremy and I know that whatever rational arguments he's going to present me with will not hold up to the fire raging in my belly. The fire I have for Dolores.

"One: for as long as I've known you, you've been straight. Two: you're thirty years old, she's what? Mid fifties? Three: she's Ian's mother."

"Well, Captain Obvious, thank you so much for that. I really hadn't figured all that out for myself just yet. I tried, you know, but I just couldn't get there without your esteemed help."

"I'm just being realistic, because you might know all these things, but I don't think they really get through to you. Or you've obviously been ignoring them."

"Maybe," I admit. "But why wouldn't I?"

"Look," Jeremy shuffles uneasily in his seat, which is not his style, "Ian dying is a very hard fact to accept. If I remember correctly, I was the one who told you to just go for it with Dolores if it made you feel even the tiniest bit better about yourself, but I never thought it would last this long and that you'd be fingering each other in the pantry while you have a crowd of guests visiting for Ian's birthday, or that you'd go to work for her in the gallery. I know this is hard for you to see because you're too enmeshed in it, because it's happening to *you*, but as an outsider, as someone looking at you from the sidelines, and greatly caring about you *and* Dolores, it's my duty to tell you what it really looks like. I think it has gone too far, Soph. I wouldn't be sitting here saying this to you if I didn't honestly believe that."

I shake my head and give him the steeliest look I can muster. "I know exactly what it looks like from the outside, but Dolores and I have taken this further than just companionship while mourning. Much further."

"Okay, okay." Jeremy shows his palms in defeat—I think. "But just so you know, I'm not *only* playing devil's advocate here. I'm genuinely concerned about you. I don't want you to get hurt even more, because, and I know you're very much aware of this, the world we live in is far from the ideal one you're dreaming of."

"I know." I give in just a little, not just to make sure Jeremy knows I am truly hearing him, but also because I do know. "But what am I supposed to do? Leave the house? Go back home? Live on my own?"

"Yes, at some point, you will have to do these things. There are no two ways about it."

"I can't leave her. The mere thought of it makes me sick to my stomach. I can't go back to Dolores and I being just mother and daughter-in-law."

"Maybe not yet." Jeremy swirls the brandy in his glass.

*Maybe not ever*, I want to say, but don't, because I know how preposterous it would sound.

# CHAPTER TWENTY-SIX

● ● ● ● ● ● ● ● ● ● ● ● ● ● ● ● ● ●

I've been helping out at Dolores' galleries for weeks now, basically spending all of my time with her. Today, Dolores takes me to meet an artist for lunch. A flighty woman called Jennifer Bloom who makes textile prints. After lunch, we decide to go home—to Dolores' house.

In the car, a U2 song comes on, and it takes me right back to a road trip Ian and I took along the Pacific Coast Highway two years ago. He used to make long playlists of which half the songs were by U2. We had a rule that whoever was driving could choose the music and he always insisted on taking the wheel.

Dolores looks at me as if she knows exactly what the song is doing to me.

"He and Angela shared a great but not entirely understandable love for all things U2. She went to their concert with him and Ethan not long before her final diagnosis. She talked about it for weeks."

"They have some good songs, I guess." I remember Ian tapping his fingers on the steering wheel while he sang along exuberantly. "This is not one of them." I don't even know the name of the song that's playing. Bono seems to repeat the words *sweetest* and *thing* often, so I guess that might be the title.

Then my phone rings. It's a number I don't recognize. If I was alone, I probably wouldn't pick up, but as though I have something to prove to Dolores by doing so, I answer.

"Hello, Miss Winters," a woman says. "This is Officer Bale with the Chicago PD. Is this a good time to talk?"

I remember Officer Bale. She's the family liaison officer they sent to see me after delivering the news of Ian's death. "Yes." My heart starts hammering. The last call I got from the CPD ruined my life.

"We've had a request from a Mister Albert Davis to contact you, asking if you'd be willing to meet him. He's the driver of the truck involved in the accident of Ian Holloway."

For an instant, it seems as though my heart might stop beating. "What does he want?" I snap.

"He would like to meet you, Ma'am. Express his condolences and convey an apology."

"An apology?" My voice rises. "What the hell am I supposed to do with that?"

"There's no need to give me an answer straight away," the police officer says. "Think about it and let me know. But, in my experience, this can be a good thing. It has been known to bring closure. Of course, you're in no way obligated to honor Mr. Davis' request. It's only a question. What happens next is totally up to you."

"Yeah. Okay," I mumble into the receiver. "I'll think about it." When I hang up, I stare at the phone, already knowing very well what my final answer will be.

"Sophie?" Dolores asks. She doesn't have time to say anything else, because then her phone starts ringing. It's connected to the car's Bluetooth system so the ringing reverberates through the entire car.

Dolores pushes a button and says hello.

The voice coming through the speakers is the same one I just talked to. Officer Bale gives the same spiel to Dolores, who answers curtly but politely, and ends the conversation by saying she'll be in touch soon.

We've reached the house and by the time we're inside, I'm fuming.

"Who the hell does that man think he is?" I shout at no one in particular, but of course Dolores is standing next to me, so she's going to have to bear the brunt of this.

"We should talk about this," she says, in that calm voice of hers, as though she's actually considering meeting him.

"We should?" My voice is full of blame already, full of anger and pain.

"Like the officer said. It might be good for us to talk to the driver."

"Good for us? Good for him, more like. He's only doing this to ease his guilty conscience, Dolores. Can't you see that?"

"He was cleared of all fault. It was a stupid freak accident. Ian was in the wrong place at exactly the wrong time. It was a morbid twist of fate. We can't blame him any more than we do Ian for what happened."

"Are you kidding me? Are you telling me you don't blame the driver? Because I sure as hell do. If he hadn't been there, Ian would still be alive. There's no way I'm shaking that man's hand and giving him the reassurance that it's not his fault."

"You're overreacting, Sophie." Dolores stands there with her hands on her hips. She's not going to be on my side for this one.

"I am not. How can you even say that? That man's existence, and his fucking truck, are the direct cause of Ian's death."

"I think you're only saying that to make yourself feel better."

"Better? Better!" Spit flies from my mouth. "Feeling better has not really been on my to-do list of late. Fuck. I can't believe this."

"You might not want to, but I'm seriously considering meeting him."

"Why?"

"Because I *need* closure. I need it more than anger toward a man I don't even know. I want to look him in the eyes. The poor man's life is probably ruined by this as well."

I'm baffled by the words coming from Dolores' mouth. "*His* life is ruined? What about our lives? None of his family members were killed, while *your* son was."

"It was an accident." Dolores' calm facade is starting to crack. "Anyway, no need for you to come with me, but…" She pauses.

"But what?"

"You can't hide forever, Sophie."

"What's that supposed to mean?"

Dolores takes a step closer, removes her hands from her hips but doesn't bring them to my shoulders the way I expect—want—her to. She lowers her voice. "You're going to have to start your own life again some time. You've lived here for four months. You have no idea when you will go back to work. You don't know what you're going to do with the apartment. And all of that is understandable, but it's not a life. At least, it shouldn't be yours."

I want to say something, give her a snippy comeback, but my throat swells and my eyes fill. Dolores is rejecting me. She wants me out. Our little arrangement has run its course.

"Fine," I whisper. "I'll pack my things and get out."

"That's not what I mean. I don't want you to leave. I just want you to… I don't know, face up to some things. Or at least try to. Make an effort to move on."

I shake my head. "I've heard enough. This has gone on long enough, anyway. It needs to stop. You're right. I'll be out of your hair as soon as possible." I start making my way toward the stairs. There's nothing but red mist in my head. Nothing but that brutal first sting of rejection. Our affair that brought me so much comfort is coming to an abrupt halt.

Dolores comes after me and grabs me by the wrist. "Don't do this, Sophie. Don't run away from yet another confrontation."

Vexed, I turn around, look her straight in the eyes.

"Another?" I manage to say.

"Please, calm down. Let's sit and talk about this like the adults we are."

"I don't need to sit for that. Just give it to me. Tell me everything you think I'm doing wrong." Now it's betrayal I feel. Dolores has never criticized me for anything. She has always been there for me one hundred percent.

"You're in a state. You're no longer thinking straight. We'll continue this later."

"No, just let me have it. Let me know what you really think. After all, we share a bed. I'm entitled to your true opinion of me."

I can tell my unwillingness to back down is riling her up. "You can't just sit by idly and wait for life to become okay again. It doesn't work like that. You need to do *something*. You need to take some sort of responsibility. And for God's sake, Sophie, call your mother back once in a while."

I take a step back. "My mother? What does my mother have to do with any of this?"

"She's a perfect example of how you avoid any confrontation. She's your mother. She loves you. You're both alive. Make some effort."

"My mother is the biggest narcissist I have ever met. I told you that. You made me believe you understood. You made me believe so many things. Was it just to get me into your bed, huh, Dolores? Was that all that this was about?"

"You know very well that's not how it is. I've loved our time together, despite how it came about." There's a lot of hurt in Dolores' voice.

"Past tense. Okay." My own anger, however, will not make way for anything else. I can't get past the comment Dolores made about my mother. If she's out to hurt me, I can give as good as I get. "I *will* pack my things then as I take it you're breaking up with me." At least I have an ounce of wherewithal left, just enough to make me swallow a vile comment about Dolores not being Ian's real mother. I respect her too much for that.

Everything coils itself into knots in my stomach that I believe will never be unfurled. I've lost Dolores now as well. But I can't just up and leave, not like this. "What do you want from me?" I ask.

"I want you to learn to stand on your own two feet again. I think I might be in the way of you doing that."

"Do you want me to go?" My voice, at least, has reached a normal volume again, unlike the way my heart is pounding in my chest.

"God no. I don't ever want you to go. But I don't know what will happen if you stay. I want you to have a life. Your *own* life."

I nod, tears dangling from my eyelids. "I'll go." It's not so much that I've overstayed my welcome, I do understand that, but after what has just been said, I can't stay. It has become impossible.

"Don't go *now*. Be reasonable," Dolores says, but she still doesn't touch me, which is telling enough in its own right.

"I have no choice." I cast one more glance at Dolores. She looks so good again today, so absolutely scrumptious in her light gray skirt suit with a red silk top underneath. Her blue eyes are moist. She has taken off her glasses and they dangle from her fingers.

It's over, and we both know it.

I head up the stairs and pack whatever I can through a haze of tears. While I fill my bag and disconnect my computer screen, a new void opens in my heart. Or maybe it has been there all along, but Dolores did a good job of filling it with all her warmth and understanding and embraces.

Half an hour later, I'm in my car, on my way to Jeremy's.

# CHAPTER TWENTY-SEVEN

●●●●●●●●●●●●●●●●●●

It's only when I arrive at Jeremy's, and have unloaded my meager belongings from the car, that it really hits me. For the very first time in almost four months, I'll be sleeping alone tonight. Since Dolores and I took our sleeping arrangement to the next level, we haven't had sex every night, of course, but there was always extensive snuggling, kissing and falling asleep in each other's arms. There was always comfort in the presence of the other. I can hardly ask Jeremy if I can share his bed.

After I've told Jeremy everything in a long, teary rant, he sits me down, and says, "First, you need a good night's sleep. Tomorrow, we will come up with our battle plan for your new life." He has taken my hand in his. His skin is sweaty and nowhere near as soft as Dolores'. "You should also text her to let her know you're here with me. So she doesn't worry too much."

Stubbornly, I push my phone away from me. "You text her."

"Would you mind if I called her? Just to have a quick chat."

"You feel sorry for her."

"A little." Jeremy says it as though he's being pinched painfully at the same time.

"I've had some time to calm down, and I do feel for Dolores, because she's alone now, too. But I think some sort of rift was the only way for us to end this. And it had to end." My voice peters out at the end of the sentence, as though even my vocal chords are unsure of this conclusion.

"It had to," I repeat, more to myself than to Jeremy.

"I'll make you some tea in a second. Then we'll talk." Jeremy grabs his own phone from the table and goes into the kitchen to call Dolores.

I strain to hear what he says, but I just make out snippets like "she's safe" and "you take care". I never asked her flat out so I don't know if Dolores has someone to talk to about this, about us. I was too absorbed by what we were doing—too self-absorbed really. Maybe she'll call June and tell her all about our sordid little affair. Because that's what it feels like to me now. It's just a bitter aftertaste, like when I have a hangover. It was fun at the time, but the consequences are far less glorious.

A few minutes later Jeremy comes back into the living room with two cups of tea. I never drank tea at Dolores'. Her professional-style coffee machine was too good.

"Okay, Sophie, my sweet, sweet friend. Please don't be offended, but I have seen this coming for a while, so I have prepared for this moment."

I raise an eyebrow. "Since when?"

"Since the day you told me, of course. I'm the king of unrealistic couplings. Remember Steve the law student? And Jared the Senate hopeful?" He purses his lips together. "Sometimes you really like someone you really shouldn't, and the very fact that you shouldn't makes you like them even more. Been there, done that. What you need now is a massive distraction and…" He taps his fingers onto the table. He's actually excited about this. "Well, I took the liberty of having a conversation with Jackie O. about your future. If you don't want to do investigative anymore, we can work something out. She can use someone extra for the weekend cultural pages, and since you've been, er, into the art world lately, that could be something for you. You can have one of the desks at *The Post*'s main office and you'd have annoying colleagues and daily boring editorial meetings, the works."

"Wow. I love how you're selling that."

"You know what I mean, Soph. As for lodgings, just move in here. Come live with me. I can't promise the same perks as living with Dolores has, but I truly don't mind. I like having you around. I am a social butterfly, however, so I am out of the house quite often, because I have my own life to live…"

"Speaking of, what about your love life? What if you want to bring a guy over?"

"Then I will." He shrugs. "There's a bathroom between our bedrooms. And I'm not that loud, anyway," Jeremy says matter-of-factly. "Besides, I no longer sleep with people who don't have their own, very comfortable digs. No more college students or married men for me. I'm so past that."

I give him a small but genuine laugh. "You really do have this all figured out."

"It may be a long time before your life feels normal again, Soph, but I think it would be a good strategy to fake it until you make it." He peers at me over the rim of his tea cup. "What do you say? Will you come to the office with me tomorrow? We can have lunch with Jackie."

"You and Jackie seem very chummy."

"It's always a good idea to keep the boss close." He cocks his head. "Is that a yes?"

"Okay." Maybe both Jeremy and Dolores are right. Either way, it's highly unlikely that two people who have my best interests at heart would both be wrong.

"Excellent. Now, guess who I'm interviewing for my podcast tonight." His eyes sparkle.

"I honestly have no idea."

"Vasily Cooke, the gorgeous artist whose work is on display in the Dolores Flemming Gallery at this very moment."

"And I thought you came to the opening to give me moral support."

"I'm self-employed, Sophie, darling. I must always have

an eye open for new business."

"Thank you." I mean it from the bottom of my heart, though it does sort of feel like I need to be saved all over again.

"You'd do the same for me." Jeremy waves me off. "I need to leave in an hour. Will you be okay on your own? I can reschedule if that would make you feel better."

"No. You should go. I have to learn to be on my own again. I might as well go cold turkey." I look around the room. Even though Jeremy has a lot of art on display, his apartment is the polar opposite of Dolores' house. For starters, it's pristine. No magazines lying around. No empty wine glasses to be found on the coffee table. It's also modern with lots of ceiling spots shining indirect light on us, angular objects and bright colors. It would fit nicely in any lifestyle magazine on interior decorating, but it's not cozy like Dolores' house.

Oh, Dolores.

"Dolores said something pretty mean about me and my mother." It helps to focus on the one thing she said that really hurt me. All the other things she said, I can understand now that I've had some time to calm down, but that particular remark still hurts.

"What did she say about the mighty Deborah Winters?" Jeremy asks.

"That I should call my mother back once in a while and that my relationship with her is a prime example of how I avoid confrontation."

"Ouch." Jeremy goes to refill my cup. "Do you need a shot of whiskey in that?"

"That was so below the belt. I can't believe she actually said that after everything I told her."

"She was upset. People say all sorts of things they don't mean when they're upset."

"That might be so, but… well, I guess I don't know how to move forward with Dolores after this. I don't want to lose her entirely. Fuck, at times, I never wanted things to end between us."

"I know." Jeremy's voice shoots up. "You sat in that very chair telling me all about your dreams for you and Dolores."

"I kind of miss her already, even though I'm also still cross with her."

"That might be so, but I do think it would be best for you not to see her for a little while. Wouldn't want you to relapse." Jeremy looks at his watch.

We sit in silence for a few seconds.

"Any chance of a hug before you leave?" I give Jeremy my most sheepish smile.

"Of course, darling, but don't get any ideas in your head for in the middle of the night."

# CHAPTER TWENTY-EIGHT

● ● ● ● ● ● ● ● ● ● ● ● ● ● ● ● ● ● ●

After Jeremy has left and I'm truly alone, I rehash everything Dolores has said. I quickly realize there's not much point, nor is there a lot of sense to me sitting in Jeremy's living room, waiting for him to come home. I stare out of the window with its scenic view over the high rises of Chicago and I know, perhaps for the first time, that I'm going to have to find a way to make it in this life alone. I'm going to have to find another reason to smile in the morning. I'm going to have to find satisfaction from something other than Dolores' hands all over me.

Dolores' hands. Dolores' lips. Dolores' post-orgasmic grin.

I grab my purse and head out for a long walk. Summer has officially descended on Chicago, but it's not too humid just yet. I have a vague destination in mind, even though it's quite a few miles from Jeremy's apartment. But it's closer than the cemetery, which is on Dolores' side of town. I walk and I walk, until it's dark, until I arrive at my destination. Cooley's.

By the time I plop down on a bar stool, I've exhausted not only the soles of my feet, but also whatever mechanism in my brain I'm using to keep my thoughts off Dolores. Perhaps my choice of bar has something to do with that. When we came here after meeting the lawyer about Ian's will, it was the first time I felt really close to her. It was also when I told her about my not-so-stellar relationship with my parents and my mother in particular. Maybe I shouldn't have told her that. There are some things certain people can't understand.

Dolores, as Ian's mother, can't really understand the complicated feelings I have for my own mother, the reasons I have for ignoring her and for not respecting her the way a daughter should. Although I think of my mother often— much more than I would like. I see her face every time I look in the mirror. I hear her voice, that shrill instrument with which she used to tell me that, no matter what, we would always be family.

*Am I as self-involved as my mother?* I ask myself while I dive into the beer I've ordered. Tommy hasn't spotted me yet, and I'm glad to have a few more minutes to myself, because he's sure to come over and give me a hug and say how sorry he is again. That's all well and good and according to the rules of mourning, but if I had a nickel for every time someone expressed to me how sorry they were since Ian died, I'd be rich. But I am already rich. Ian took care of that. Though I can honestly say that money has never been a motivator for anything in my life. On the contrary. All the money my mother made while she was out running her company and missing our childhood never did a thing to make my brother and me happier. I knew from the age of six that money doesn't bring happiness. It bought us a parade of nannies, that's it.

I toy with my phone and it's so hard not to text Dolores. We'd be having dinner right about this time. Who is she having dinner with? Did our affair awaken a new longing inside of her? Did it make her ready to explore relationships again? Any woman who gets her will be the luckiest woman on the planet, I conclude, but don't text her. I have to be strong. But not so strong that I can't knock back my beer in a few large gulps.

Then Tommy spots me. He comes over, embraces me and tells the bartender not to charge me for anything. Story of my life. Wanting to pay for every little thing and never having to. Except for the one thing that money can't buy.

Love. I'm paying for that big time. I pay for Ian's death with loneliness. With giving up my affair with his mother.

Tommy is called back behind the bar and as soon as he leaves, I compose a text to Dolores, but I don't send it. Not yet.

*Get a grip*, I tell myself. I delete the message. A relapse so soon would be fatal. There have been enough fatalities.

By the time I've downed my third beer, I can almost see Ian sitting on the bar stool next to me, like some alcohol-induced hallucination—though I've become used to much stronger beverages than beer by now. I see him leaning his elbows on the bar, dividing his attention between a football game on the television mounted on the wall, exchanging quips with Tommy, and talking to me.

I blink a few times, until I don't see him anymore. But no longer seeing him hasn't stopped me from missing him. I order another beer, because I don't want to go back to Jeremy's. God knows what he and Vasily are up to. I blink, wanting to see Ian again. I can imagine him, of course. His pitch black hair. His dark eyes. His long limbs always spilling over all the furniture. And I want to ask him: "What should I do, Ian? Should I meet that wretched driver? Will that change anything? And what on earth am I going to do about Dolores?"

Good thing I'm drunk because I'm of half a mind to take a detour past her house, see what she's up to. I wasn't meant to be missing two people. One was more than enough.

I call a taxi and finish my drink. Inside the taxi, I give the driver Jeremy's address.

# CHAPTER TWENTY-NINE

●●●●●●●●●●●●●●●●●●●●

It's 3 a.m. and I can't sleep, so I grab my phone from the nightstand and log on to Facebook. Everyone else's lives seem to be moving along as swiftly as ever. When I open the Mail app, my heart skips a beat. There's an email from Dolores. Sent about an hour ago. I guess she can't sleep either. With trembling hands I scroll through it.

*Sophie,*

*I want you to know that I'm meeting Mr. Davis next Saturday at 2 p.m. at the Starbucks on North Michigan Avenue. You are welcome to join me. My reasons for wanting to meet with him are my own. You make your own decision. Whatever you decide is up to you and will not be subject to judgment from me.*

*I'm sorry you felt you had to leave so abruptly. I never wanted that.*

*Love,*

*Dolores*

It's the word *Love* that gets me the most. There's no chance of me getting any more sleep now. But staying at Jeremy's is different. I can't just roam around the apartment in the middle of the night. It's too small for that. Everything was different at Dolores', easier. Her warm woman smell when I spooned her before falling asleep. The sweet nothings she whispered in my ear upon waking. Having slept by her side for all those weeks makes this so much more unbearable.

This cold place in the bed next to me. I remember what I said to Jeremy that day when I was playing make-believe, when I was dreaming of an ideal world in which Dolores and I could be together. How I'd defended our doomed affair as I tried to put into words that she and I could be a viable couple. He was right and I was wrong.

That doesn't mean I don't want to see her.

I put my phone down and surrender to the darkness of the night again. Just me and my thoughts. So much has happened since I last slept alone. Time has passed, for starters. Perhaps it's this room, because it's the one I slept in right after Ian's accident, but I get a clear sense that I shouldn't be staying here anymore. That if I'm going to do this on my own, I should really be alone and not use Jeremy as my crutch to make the transition bearable. I've used Dolores for that purpose long enough already.

I need to go home and really face what has happened. I need to sort through his clothes and shoes and papers, through his artworks on the walls, and give away whatever I don't want to keep as a memento. I need to make our place *my* place. I need to move on.

\* \* \*

*Ian,*

*I've decided to move back home. It's been more than four months now. Four months… can you even believe it? The world has been without you for four entire months. I don't even know how that is possible. Death is just so cruel and final. One second you're there, drawing breath, the next you're gone. It can all be over in an instant. Maybe that's why I've been clinging to Dolores so hard. First, it made me feel less dead inside, like I actually wanted to continue living without you. And now, while I'm scribbling this in Jeremy's guest room, it makes me realize that life is so precious. What if I walk out of here tomorrow and it's my turn? My number is up and I get mowed down by one of those SUVs that don't belong in the city center—your words. What will I have to show for my life?*

Granted, I lost my way, and I surely haven't found it yet. But I did lose myself a little in the affair with your mother, and I get what she was trying to say when we had that fight. That was another gift Dolores gave me. The gift of showing me what I was doing to myself, how I was stifling me, and us—her and me. It's funny that us no longer means you and me, Ian. I belong to another us now. Well, not really. I guess we broke up, if that's even a thing. I'm not sleeping with your mother anymore. If you weren't dead, I'd say you could resume breathing normally again. (Did I just make a joke about you dying? That's a first.)

The fact is that you're gone and I remain. I need to pull myself together and I know how I'm going to do it. It could be that I need to stop writing you these letters, but I've grown quite fond of writing them. It doesn't hurt me so much anymore that you will never read them. In fact, after some of the things I've written, I'm glad you never will.

I'm moving home and I'm going back to work. I'm returning to my old self. Well, I'll never be my old self again—you changed me forever. Not only because you died. But you had already changed me so much while you were alive. Those six years we had together, though surely too short, improved my personality vastly. I'm not so bitter anymore. Not so angry all the time. I don't feel like such a victim, anymore. Though for a while, after the accident, I did feel like the greatest martyr on the planet. 'Why me' is a pretty automatic thought under the circumstances, I'd like to think so, but I'm not certain because Dolores never seemed to suffer from it. That was one of the things that really drew me to her. Dolores is not a victim. Not after Angela's death and not after yours.

I miss her. Maybe I shouldn't write that in this letter to you, but I miss her. Her proximity gave me something extra, the edge I needed to make it through the day in the beginning, and so much more afterwards. We brought each other joy in a dark, hopeless time. For that, I will always be grateful to her. She saved me, of that I'm sure. She saved me once and then she saved me again.

I've been strong. I haven't contacted her. I've been here for four days now and I've resisted the urge, because every time I picture Dolores reading a needy message from me, I imagine her rolling her eyes at a person I don't want to be. At this moment, I don't really know what person exactly I want to be to her. But I will start by being someone who will, with her, face the guy whose truck made you lose your balance that day. We've taken some big steps together already, and I feel, in my heart of hearts, though I can't really put it into words, that I need to do this with her as well. It's part of our journey together.

But I have no idea what I'm going to say to that man. Most certainly, in my head, it is his fault, even though my rational mind knows that it's not. He was perfectly within his rights to back into the street—he was about to make a delivery to Origino, where you stopped sometimes after work to pick up organic kale. Can I really be angry at a man who delivers organic produce for a living?

I think my lack of sleep is making me a little delirious. Does anything that I've written here make sense at all, babe? I miss calling someone babe. It's just a stupid word, but I miss calling you that. I can't sleep, Ian. Not yet. I doze and have these crazy dreams about everything all together and then when I wake up I'm convinced for a second that they were real, and there's no one in my bed to tell me that they're not.

I miss you.

Sophie

# CHAPTER THIRTY

● ● ● ● ● ● ● ● ● ● ● ● ● ● ● ● ● ● ●

The day I move back home is the first really hot one of the summer. Sweat runs down my back as I haul my computer back into my office. Everything in the apartment feels like it belongs to a former life. Jeremy offered to help me move, but I told him it was something I needed to do on my own.

The first thing I do after finding a spot for my stuff, which is easy because I just put everything back where it came from, is give the place a good scrub. Neither Ian nor I were very big on housework and soon after moving in together we decided it was of vital importance to our relationship to hire someone to come and clean a few times a week. I refused to pick up his haphazardly discarded socks and he wasn't going to do the same for me.

Though I fully intend to get our cleaner to come back, I somehow feel I need to be the one to remove the dust that has gathered since his death. It's some sort of symbolic gesture—wiping away old dirt before I can start messing up the place again on my own.

This particular activity takes me throughout the entire flat. I run my fingers over every last object. The model of the Sydney Opera House he made in Lego. The Rubik's cube he never managed to solve because he refused to look up how to do it on the internet. A stack of *Architectural Digest* magazines he insisted on keeping. His laptop. A frame with a picture of him, Angela, and Dolores.

I remember when, on our first date, he told me he had an absent father in England, and he had two mothers. I thought I hid my initial shock well by acting all enlightened about it, but he later told me it was very visible on my face. Oh, the irony, I think now, as I clean off this particular picture frame with extra zeal.

Of course, I can't sleep, but lying in our bed, in some ways, is more bearable than tossing and turning in Jeremy's spare bed. It's something that I need to do, whereas staying at Jeremy's meant postponing this even longer, felt like marking time.

The first few days and nights are long, and I make sure I'm out of the apartment as much as possible during the day. I set up a meeting with Jackie O'Brien and get myself set up to start work soon. I visit Alex who is on bed rest for a few days and is going mad, but whose gaze softens when it lands on me. All the while, I try not to think about Dolores and her email. I don't reply, fearing that if I do, I won't be able to stop myself from saying something I don't want to. I don't know what I want. I miss her. There's no doubt about that, but I need to figure out which parts of her I miss. Do I miss comforting, strong Dolores? Or do I really miss *her*, elegant, successful, gorgeous Dolores? The two are so intertwined that I can't come to a conclusion.

Was my affair with her solely a means of getting through those first four months?

Does she miss me?

All these questions run through my head on repeat as I lie awake in the bed I used to share with Ian. Every morning I hope to find the answer, to get a sign from somewhere, but my brain is muddled by lack of sleep, and missing Dolores' arms around me. I want so many things to be different that I don't know where one desire begins and the other ends anymore.

Every day, I stand with my phone in my hand, ready to call her. But I can't bring myself to do it because there is no going back. No going back to the me of three, or even two months ago, when I was so much more devastated than I am now. And a part of me is afraid. What if I were to be with her again, but the comfort she provides, the warmth, the *love*, what if they're still there but I don't feel them anymore? "At least I had that," I mutter to myself. At least, underneath all the rage and the sadness and the pointlessness, she made me feel things. What if I see her and it's all gone and it's all revealed for exactly what it was: a sham. A means to forget. A drug I was temporarily addicted to. A cheap thrill. A perversion I lost myself in so readily—and what would that say about me now? Then our time together would lose its luster.

All the while, Ian is still dead, never to return, and I have a life to get back to. An existence to build without Ian. A hole in my heart to fill—as opposed to merely stopping the bleed with the temporary fix of Dolores' affection.

But sometimes, in my most unguarded moments, a smile wells in my chest when I think of Dolores entering the bedroom in her tank top and shorts, of how she hummed along to the *Grace & Frankie* theme tune. I watched a couple of episodes in the middle of the night two days ago because I couldn't sleep and it made me feel closer to her.

And so, on Saturday morning, when I wake from the light slumber I usually drift into in the early hours, groggy and tears at the ready, I know what I'm going to do. How will I ever find out what we really have between us if I keep ignoring Dolores?

# CHAPTER THIRTY-ONE

●●●●●●●●●●●●●●●●●●●●

When I see her, I know I made the right decision to come. I'm at the Starbucks thirty minutes early, but Dolores is already there. I look at her from the door, again wondering why we're doing this at a Starbucks of all places. Maybe the driver suggested it and Dolores went along with it because she's an easy-going person. Or perhaps she's expecting me to come and thought a Starbucks on a Saturday afternoon in this part of town—a very public place—would curb any too dramatic outbursts from me.

I didn't tell her I was coming. I wanted to give myself every opportunity to back out at the last minute without disappointing her with a late cancellation. Now I'm here, and I look at her perched at the table, reading something on her iPad—probably *The Chicago Morning Post*—and I'm glad I came. If only to see her. Because my heart does that silly pitter-patter of excitement already.

As though she senses my presence, Dolores looks up and our gazes cross. And it's like something out of a movie. All the other patrons freeze, cease to exist entirely, and Dolores is my only focus. I'm frozen in time too, in that perfect moment when she spots me, before any words can spoil this reunion, before the driver turns up and adds a bunch of emotions I'm pretty sure I won't know how to deal with. I see her, and I know.

She pushes her glasses up the bridge of her nose and the world slips into focus again. I don't go to her immediately; I want to savor this moment of anticipation, these few minutes during which everything is still possible. I order a cappuccino which will be vastly inferior to anything Dolores' state-of-the-art coffee machine produces, wait for it at the counter, then join her.

Then I don't know what to say. I'm brimming with emotions already. I should have met with her privately first. But I couldn't foresee it was going to be like this, that just seeing her again would turn my voice into a stammer, would turn my entire body into a stuttering mess. That is not what today is about. But it feels as though, since I left Dolores' house last week, and took the first small steps to getting my life back on track, I've kept a lid on my feelings for her—and now they just want to burst out.

"Sophie." Dolores rises, squeezes my shoulder with all the tenderness in the world, and presses a kiss on my cheek. "You came."

I nod and sit next to her, turning my body so I can look at her. I ignore the coffee. My stomach won't agree with it anyway. Who needs coffee when you have Dolores Flemming sitting next to you?

"I'm glad," she says. "I think it's important." She clears her throat. "When you didn't reply to my email, I wasn't sure what to expect."

I can't tell her that sending even the shortest reply would have put me in jeopardy of saying too much, of pouring my heart out to her with words instead of deeds, in a way we're not accustomed to. "It was kind of a last-minute decision."

"How are you feeling?" She peers at me over her glasses.

"You know." I have so much to say to her, but there's no time, and this is not the place. "You?"

"I understand your initial reluctance to this better now that the moment is here." She gives me a small smile. "Look, Sophie, I said some things…"

I hold up my hand. "It's okay. You said some things I needed to hear."

Can she tell that all I want to do is kiss her? Should we just get out of here, forget the truck driver, and go to her house?

"I also said some things I didn't mean. I need you to know that. I was upset. That phone call had upset me. It..." The door opens and we both look up. A young man walks in with skateboard in hand.

"How will we know it's him?" I'm hit by a bout of nerves, making me inappropriately giggly about this situation.

"Officer Bale will be joining us. She knows who we are." Dolores' voice trembles.

"I'm nervous."

"It's normal." Under the table, Dolores' hand comes to rest on my thigh. "It's last-minute jitters. It'll pass once he's here." Her hand travels down and she gives my knee a squeeze.

The door opens again and a man walks in with two women by his side. Although she's not in uniform, I recognize Officer Bale. She spots us and they walk over.

Dolores' hand slips off my leg. She rises and I follow her example. Am I really meant to shake that man's hand? Will it achieve anything if I refuse?

Officer Bale makes the introductions and offers to get coffee for everyone. The second woman is Albert's wife Ginny. Albert is skinny, pale, with dark circles underneath his eyes. He looks so regular, so like every other man in his age bracket you'd see walking down the street. But he also looks like a man suffering greatly from having put his truck in reverse one fatal day.

We shake hands—his is sweaty and limp—and sit.

"Thank you for agreeing to meet with me." Surprisingly, Albert is able to look us both in the eyes. He looks at me first, then at Dolores. "It must be really difficult. I really appreciate it."

Next to me, Dolores hums something inaudible. I just

nod once.

"I want you to know that the accident has had a profound effect on my life as well. I haven't been able to sleep properly, haven't been eating. I feel responsible for what happened. I... saw him after he fell. I tried to help, but he was—"

His wife puts a hand on his arm. "We're in no way comparing our grief to yours, but I guess we both wanted you to know that we live with what happened every day too. It haunts us. It's not something you can shake off. You can't pick yourself up and move on. Al hasn't been driving. He hasn't found the confidence to get back behind the wheel."

*Good*, I think. Let *Al* suffer. Let him never set foot in a car again. Maybe he should get a bike and feel vulnerable in traffic for a change.

Officer Bale returns with a tray of coffee cups. She pulls up a chair, but doesn't say anything.

"I'm so very sorry," Albert says. "I've replayed the moment in my head so many times, thinking what I could possibly have done differently. I parked in that street every other day."

"You didn't hit him," Dolores says. "You didn't do anything wrong." Dolores' voice is icy.

"I know that technically and, according to the law, I didn't." Albert casts a glance at Officer Bale. "But that doesn't mean I don't feel like I'm to blame regardless."

"What do you want us to say?" It's my turn to speak. I keep my voice low out of respect for Dolores, because I know she would want me to. "That we absolve you of your guilt?"

Dolores clears her throat.

"No. Absolutely not," Albert says. "I imagine that's why you would think I asked to meet, but all I want to do is apologize and express my condolences for your loss in person. No matter how I twist or turn it, I had a hand in Ian's accident. If I hadn't been there at that time, it probably wouldn't have happened. I wanted to look you in the eye and let you know that I don't take that lightly."

"We appreciate the gesture." My tone is all sarcasm, though I do feel for him a little.

"It's hard for all of us," Albert's wife says.

"I don't think there's anything left to say." Dolores shuffles noisily in her seat, as though she's making to get up, but doesn't.

"I understand. I just wanted to tell you, face-to-face, that I'm sorry. I felt I owed you that at least." Albert's hand is trembling as he reaches for his coffee cup.

He was the last person to see Ian. Maybe he saw him in his rearview mirror and Ian was still alive. Then the next time Albert saw him, Ian was dead.

"Thank you, Albert. It means, er…" I can hardly say it means a lot.

"We should probably go now." His wife pushes her chair back.

No handshakes are exchanged. Only a few slight nods, a couple of averted glances, and Albert and his wife go out the door. Officer Bale sticks around for a few minutes, thanking us for our time and telling us to call her if we need anything at all.

"That was weird," I say when it's just Dolores and me.

Dolores sits there shaking her head. "It was. I can't quite put it into words yet." She scrunches her lips together.

Her complexion is paler than usual. Her eyes a bit watery.

"Do you want to talk about it?" I ask.

She shrugs. "It was near insignificant to meet that man. I was hoping for some cathartic moment, but it was the exact opposite." She stares in front of her. "In the end, it still wasn't his fault. And Ian is still dead."

# CHAPTER THIRTY-TWO

●●●●●●●●●●●●●●●●●●●

"I would really like to talk to you about something else. Not here. In private. We can go to my place, if you like."

"Your place?" Dolores turns to me.

"I've moved back home. I'm no longer at Jeremy's."

She nods, remains silent for a couple of long seconds, then says, "I'd feel more comfortable going to my house."

Five minutes later, we're in her car. She turns on the radio. I'm guessing she needs some time without conversation to process the meeting with Albert. As for me, I'm frantically trying to arrange the jumble of words in my head. I've not planned for this. I know *what* I want to say but I have no idea how to make it plausible, how to translate what's in my heart into acceptable sentences.

"When did you move back?" she asks after a while.

"Last week. I love Jeremy dearly but staying at his apartment is not, er, the same. And I had to go back at some point."

"Is it not too hard?"

I glance at Dolores' profile. She has her eyes firmly fixed on the road. I can't gauge how she's feeling, as though a week and a half apart has already put an impenetrable distance between us and what we had together was very much based on proximity and opportunity. I do sense that Dolores is close to falling apart, that the meeting with the driver has unsettled her more than she's letting on.

Or maybe I'm the one having an unnerving effect on her.

"It has its hard moments." I want to talk about this but

I have other, more pressing things I want to tell her first. "Returning home was never going to be a walk in the park."

Dolores parks shoddily in front of her house. My suspicion that she is very upset is confirmed. A drizzle is falling and we hurry inside. She takes my coat as though I didn't live there for months and have suddenly forgotten where the coat rack is.

I follow her into the kitchen. She's the least composed I've ever seen her. She clatters coffee cups about, tries to refill the machine with water but her hands tremble too much.

"Hey." I put a hand on her elbow. "Please, sit. Let me take care of making coffee." I want to take her in my arms and help her get through this moment, but I'm sure she wouldn't let me. Not yet.

We sit around the kitchen table, its surface a safe barrier between us.

"What did you want to talk about?" Dolores rests her glance on me for a split second before it skitters away again.

I think she knows why I'm here. But before I tell her in my own words, I need to know how she's holding up. To see her like this, her glance flitting about, like she doesn't know where to look—like she can barely look me in the eye.

"Let's talk about you first." I try to find her eyes.

Dolores shakes her head. "Not now. I want to hear what you have to say."

"Okay." I clear my throat. Pause. Try to gather my thoughts, which have become even more scattered at the sight of Dolores crumbling. But I have to say this now. This is my chance. "The past week has been one of the hardest since Ian died," I begin. "You can probably guess why." This is no time to be coy, I admonish myself inwardly. Just tell it like it is. "But I've tried to... remedy some of the things you, er, said I should. Just tiny steps. I moved back into the apartment. I slept in our bed, though sleep is perhaps too big a word for the tossing and turning I've been doing. I watched television from the spot on the couch where we used to lay curled up together. I drank coffee from his mug. I made my own breakfast. Just cereal, by the way. Nothing fancy like you used to make for me and… I sat down with the editor-in-chief of *The Post*. I'll be working for the weekend cultural supplement. Part-time, but it means I'll have a work place to go to on a regular basis, people to see, responsibilities. I want to go back to investigative journalism as well. Jackie begged me to not give that up, and when Jackie O. begs…" I chuckle uncomfortably. "The point is that I'm starting to pull myself together. I'm beginning to reconstruct a life. A life I can imagine living, except for one thing."

Dolores has her eyes on me now. I continue. "At first I didn't allow myself to. I told myself I was crazy, that this was for the best and all that bullshit, but damn it, Dolores, I have missed you so much. Seeing you again today… I just knew. I've known it all along. Otherwise why would I have even done it? Why would I have gone to bed with you if I didn't really want you? Because I do. I want you. I want to… I don't know. Try." My palms have gone clammy and a trickle of sweat drips down my spine, resting in the hollow at the small of my back. Now it's my turn to look away. "If that's what you want as well, of course."

I can hear Dolores expel a deep breath. "You want to try what exactly?"

"I want us to try, Dolores. Date. Whatever you want to call it."

"You want to date me?" There's a note of incredulity in Dolores' voice but also a tiny smile breaking on her lips.

"Yes, but, you know, properly. I don't want to live in your house. I don't want you to take care of me. I don't want you to hide me away from the real world." I try to loosen my limbs a little, not wring my hands so frantically.

"You want to be my *girlfriend*?" She really laughs now. It's not an accepting sort of laugh; it's definitely a sneering one.

"When you put it like that, it sounds ridiculous. But what we had was never ridiculous to me. It was beautiful and exhilarating and comforting. It was many things, but never ridiculous or... deserving of that derisive snort you just gave."

"Sophie, honey, I'm not mocking you. Not at all. Please don't for a second think I haven't entertained the notion myself, but you must see that it's not feasible."

"How can we know if we don't try?" Dolores' reluctance doesn't deter me. Being so close to her—I can grab her hand any time, feel her skin against mine any second—renews the fervor inside of me. "I know it's unorthodox, but I, at least, feel like we owe it to ourselves to try. I'm very much aware of all the arguments against us doing so and I will happily give you my reasons why we should try regardless. I haven't lost my mind. On the contrary. I want you. I don't mean I want what you gave me when I was at my lowest. I want what you can give me now that I've re-entered life. Because that's what it's all about for me now. We have one life. We *still* have it, unlike the people we love. I want you, it's as simple as that. I'm alive and I want you. Fuck all the rest. It's not important, at least too unimportant not to try." I pause to take a much-needed breath. "I truly hope that I'm not imagining things, that what we had between us was something you wanted too. Us being together. The companionship. The simple fact of no longer being alone."

"You make a compelling case." Dolores sucks her bottom lip into her mouth.

I don't want to give her too much time to think. I want to overwhelm her with reasons to do this, to choose me, no matter how much her common sense is rallying against it.

"I know what you're thinking and I'm thinking the same." I hold up my fingers, just as I did when I tried to explain my feelings to Jeremy, glad that I had the practice.

"I'm not a lesbian, the age difference is too big, and you're Ian's mother. Those are the three big ones. I'm well aware. I won't claim I can reason them all away, but this is not about reason in the first place. This is about how I feel for you, Dolores. Yes, you're Ian's mother, but that's what brought us together. And it's true that I've never before been attracted to a woman, but I am now. You know that. You've witnessed it. I've fallen for you, big time. No, I haven't just fallen for you. I love you. Not only because of how good you've been to me, how kind and generous, but because of who you are. Because of everything you stand for. And the age difference, well, you're fifty-six and gorgeous. I don't really have anything else for that. Do I have a crystal ball with which I can predict the future? No, I do not. All I know is that it can be all over just like that." I snap my fingers. "Just like it was for Ian. Or we could get sick, like Angela. In either case, before we draw our final breath, don't you want to have tried? To have afforded yourself this flimsy chance at happiness? A happiness so sudden, so unexpected, but happiness nonetheless. We know life is not a fairy-tale. We know it can really, really suck. Ian and Angela died. We're alive. And I want to be with you and I truly don't give a fuck what anyone else thinks about that."

"You've clearly thought this through."

I shake my head. "No, I haven't. I haven't dared to think about it. Not since I left here. But this is what's in my heart. This is what I felt when I saw you again today. I knew I had to try. I didn't prepare for this, but this is how it is."

"You're very passionate, Sophie. But, as you said earlier, I am much older than you and I can so easily predict how this will play out."

"Oh, so you do have a crystal ball?"

"No, I don't, but—"

"What have you truly got to lose?" I should probably give Dolores a chance to express her thoughts, but I'm so wrapped up in my speech, I need to get all the words out now, before they desert me again. I need to know I did my utmost. That I gave it all when I tried to win Dolores' heart. "Please know I'm not suggesting we run off and get married somewhere. One date, that's all I ask for. One simple date. We'll meet at a restaurant. We'll have dinner, some drinks. It'll all be very normal and civilized. Then we'll see how we feel."

"How can I say no to that?" Dolores cocks her head to the left. "It would just be a date, right?"

"Yes." It appears I'm all out of words now.

"When do you propose we go on this date?"

"Tonight."

Dolores chuckles. "Tonight? That doesn't leave me much time to get ready."

"You look perfect the way you are right now." Did Dolores just agree to go on a date with me? I want to jump out of my chair and kiss her, but I'd better not. It's not part of our new protocol.

"So do you. You look good. Better. Different."

"All of that on hardly any sleep." I dare to inch my fingers a little closer to hers across the table. "Imagine how I will look after a good night's rest."

She puts her palm on my fingers and I feel her touch shoot to the tiniest nerve endings in the furthest extremities of my body. "Let's not get ahead of ourselves," she says.

\* \* \*

*Ian,*

*I shouldn't be falling in love. I know that. And I certainly shouldn't be falling in love with your mother. What does it say about me that I'm about to go on a date with someone a mere four months after we buried you? But here's how I see it: I could choose to feel bad about it, to not enjoy it, to analyze it to death—because what's a little bit more of feeling bad in my life right now, anyway? Just throw it on the pile. I'll deal with it through too much alcohol and sleepless nights and looking at my worn-out face in the mirror, although Dolores said I looked good earlier today. "Better. Different." Those were her exact words. Another option is for us to wait for this to become appropriate, but the thing is that, between your mother and me, things will never be 'appropriate' all of a sudden. I admit that it's part of the appeal. But, and this is really what it's all about: I don't want to wait or feel bad about it. I consider myself lucky that I have her in my life. I don't want to censor myself and have long discussions about what's wrong or right. Wrong was you dying. Wrong was Angela getting lung cancer. Categorically. But is me going on a date—a real, proper date—with Dolores wrong? If it is, I don't see why. You might say that I can't see things clearly, but the thing is that I do. I really do. Because for the longest time, I didn't. I know the difference between the two. I feel it, too. Despite the odds stacked against us, I choose her. I'm wooing her—I'm actually wooing your mother, Ian—and she agreed to go on this date with me. I may claim it's just a date, but it's much more than that because how can it not be? We lived together for more than three months. I slept in her bed night after night. This date is not about getting to know each other better. The sole purpose of this date is to check for viability, though that sounds a bit clinical. A bit cold. While Dolores makes me feel the opposite of cold. Isn't that what it's all about? Being with someone who lifts you up? Who makes you feel like you can do so much more than you ever thought yourself capable of? That's how it was with you, Ian. Then you died. You died and all the rules changed. In a world where you can die in a matter of seconds, there are no rules I need to abide by. That's what I have learned. So, I'm going on this date. I'm wearing the teal dress. Yes, I'm going all out. I'm going to seduce your mother and I'm not going to apologize for it.*

*Sophie*

# CHAPTER THIRTY-THREE

●●●●●●●●●●●●●●●●●●●●●

I suggested going to the small Italian near Dolores' house for our date, but she insisted on trying a new place she'd read about—in *The Post* of all places.

She's already seated when I arrive and, very formally, gets up to greet and kiss me on the cheek after the hostess has shown me to our table.

"You look lovely," she says, and by the way her eyes devour me, I can tell that she means it.

"As do you." Stunning is a more accurate description of how Dolores looks in that red dress that is showing a lot more cleavage than I had expected—and makes her intentions known before we've even started this date. Her lipstick matches the color of her dress and her hair is combed loosely backward.

"I had to pull some strings to get this table at such short notice, so I thought I'd make an effort." She sends me a seductive smile.

Oh my. This is not the Dolores who sidled up to me in bed in her tank top and shorts, who stroked my neck so gently, who told me I could cry all the tears I wanted. Dolores has not come here to comfort me tonight. She has come to dazzle.

It's working.

"You're such a power lesbian." I wink at her. "I'm very lucky to be your guest at this swanky place."

"Power lesbian? Where did you get that?" She reaches for the wine menu.

"I don't know where I got it. But it's a thing. In fact,

I've had it on my list of possible long form topics for a while. I may need to bump it up. It could be my re-entry into the field of serious investigative journalism. 'Meet Chicago's Power Lesbians.' A picture of you looking like that to accompany it. Jackie O. would cream her panties."

Dolores chuckles. "I thought those kinds of fluffy pieces were beneath you?"

"What would be fluffy about that?" I look into her eyes for a few moments. "It would be deadly serious."

A waiter comes by to take our drinks order. Dolores chooses a bottle of red without asking for my input. When the waiter has gone, she leans over a little, affording me an intoxicating glimpse at her cleavage.

"Before we ramp up the flirting, I need to say something." She clears her throat. "I was out of line when I said you should call your mother. I shouldn't have said that because it's not for me to judge you on that, especially not after you confided in me about how you feel about her. I respect your feelings. I really do. I didn't mean to hurt you."

"Of all the things you said, that stung the most."

"I could have kicked myself for that one. It was just a reaction. Something that slipped out. Probably because I have just lost my son and it hurts so much and, well, it's not really the same for me. I've felt like a mother to him for a very, very long time, but I didn't give birth to him. He didn't have my genes. I had nothing to do with his conception whatsoever. I was never even able to adopt him. I'm not saying I loved him any less than Angela, but he didn't live inside of me for nine months. I wasn't there when he was born. Angela—and Ian especially—would balk if they heard me say this. It's not that I feel like less of a mother to him than Angela, but it's not *exactly* the same. It never could have been. I think that's where that comment came from. I was just imagining your mother and how the distance between the two of you must make her feel sometimes." She pauses. "I'm not sure if I'm making myself very clear, Sophie. These are all very complex feelings, with many sides to them."

"You were pissed off. I get it."

The waiter brings over the wine and makes a spectacle of having Dolores taste. She approves and by the time I'm presented with a glass, I have to stop myself from gulping it down.

Dolores raises her glass. "To us going on a date. It only took us five minutes to get into the really heavy topics." She smiles that bright, bright smile of hers. Already, I want to kiss that lipstick away. For now, I'll settle for ogling how it makes her lips look.

"Maybe we should give the topic of mothers a rest altogether." I clink the rim of my glass against hers. We drink while gazing in to each other's eyes.

"I'm sure the subject will come up again." She sets her glass down. "But one more thing on a more serious note. It was never my intention to have you leave the house that day. I truly didn't want you to leave. After you'd gone, I didn't know what to do with myself. I was at the gallery from seven in the morning until ten in the evening every day, just to wear myself out."

"I had to leave, though. It was inevitable. It had to happen."

"I see that, but... I missed you."

We haven't ordered our food yet, and already an unbearable heat travels underneath my skin. "So... if you missed me so much, why where you playing so hard to get this afternoon?"

"I wasn't playing hard to get at all." The million-dollar smile is back on Dolores' face. "It was a very emotional afternoon: meeting the truck driver and seeing you again. I didn't know what to do with myself. And, yes, perhaps I wanted you to convince me, but I certainly didn't need you to." Her hand glides across the table in search of mine. "And, boy, all those things you said."

I have no qualms whatsoever about putting my hand

on Dolores', for everyone to see. It fills me with pride to sit here with her in this posh restaurant, flirting my socks off and having her reciprocate.

"I meant every last word."

"There's no doubt in my mind that you did. You should have become a lawyer. Your arguing skills are out of this world."

"Only when I'm super passionate about the subject. I guess I could have only ever become your lawyer."

"Being a power lesbian, I could do with a lawyer."

"Are you ready to order now?" a waiter I hadn't noticed approaching asks. I haven't even glimpsed at the menu.

I ask him what the specials are and I pick something from the list he rattles off. So does Dolores. Then it's back to gazing into each other's eyes.

This date is exceeding all my expectations. What surprises me most, however, is how astoundingly little I care about how inappropriate this might be. It was easy enough to write in a letter to my dead boyfriend. A letter no one will ever read. But to sit here, with Dolores, out in public, and not give one iota, sets my blood on fire a little more still.

\* \* \*

"Do you want to come home with me?" Dolores asks after we've declined a look at the dessert menu.

"More than anything, but..." It takes every last ounce of willpower to decline Dolores' invitation.

She paints a smile on her lips. "Your turn to play hard to get?"

I shake my head. "No. It really isn't. I just think it's important for me not to end up at your house so quickly again. I'm absolutely not rejecting you, or your offer, just taking a rain check."

"So we really are going to date old-school?" Dolores rests her chin on her upturned hand and her red-varnished fingernails tap against her cheek.

"I don't see how else we can go about this." I expel a

quick sigh. "I think something should be different. Something more than having had a week and a half apart."

"So much is different already. You're putting your life back together."

"I guess I'm afraid that landing in your bed may put an abrupt halt to that and that's not something I can afford."

"Hey." She drops her hand on the table and scoots it closer to mine. "I understand." She slants her head a little. "So? When is our next *proper* date?" Dolores' pinkie finger has reached mine and they only have to brush against each other faintly for me to feel it everywhere.

"Tomorrow?" I offer. "Coffee?"

"Coffee it is." Dolores broadens her smile. "This date went well," she says. "So well, in fact, that I totally forgot to feel bad about it."

"Hm." I lean over the table. "What is this... thing between us? It's glorious, but I can't explain it."

"Some things can't be explained." She gives a little chuckle, bites her bottom lip.

"Thank you for coming out with me tonight."

"I think dating is a good idea."

"*Properly* dating." I pause while the check is being deposited on the table. "Have you told anyone about us?"

"No, but I think James suspects something. That man knows me too well."

"So you didn't have anyone to talk to about what happened?"

"I contemplated telling June, but, I don't know. I guess I didn't want to ruffle any feathers before I knew... how things would play out between us."

"Are you going to tell her?"

"In due course."

I wave off Dolores' attempt to pay for the meal and put my credit card on the tray with the check.

"If she's anything like Jeremy, you'd best have some very strong arguments at the ready."

"The tiniest flicker of happiness is the strongest argument possible in this case." Dolores grabs my hand again.

\* \* \*

Outside the restaurant, we stand around, weighing our options while a mild summer breeze ruffles the fabric of Dolores' dress. Have I lost my mind rejecting what she just offered? Not going home with her tonight? But it's one of these things I instinctively know not to give in to. I'm not myself enough yet to risk losing myself again. If I end up in her bed tonight, that's what will happen.

It has also been a long, exhausting day. I might actually sleep tonight.

Dolores puts a hand on my shoulder. "Will you be okay?"

"I will be."

"There's a cab coming over there." She looks out onto the street behind me.

"Just let it pass." I pull her closer by the wrist. "There will be another one soon enough."

"On a Saturday night in this part of town?" She leans in, her lips so close I can almost taste them.

"Then we'll just stand here for a while longer." I close my eyes and press my lips against hers.

# CHAPTER THIRTY-FOUR

Before I meet Dolores for coffee the next day, I go through more of Ian's things. Before he trained as an architect and started using straight lines and measured angles for everything, he was quite the sketch artist. In a folder in one of the closets we hardly ever opened, I find a bunch of his drawings from before we met. One is of a car. Not an actual car, but a futuristic model with something that looks like wings, all sleek lines and nerd aspirations. Another one is a self-portrait that didn't turn out very well. I can see his resemblance in the picture he drew, but some of his features, like his nose, are just off enough to confuse me.

It's funny that, while he did often mention he loved to draw, in all the time we were together, I never once saw him do it, not free-hand. It makes me think about the endless variations of a person, of how I probably brought out different things in him than his ex-girlfriend Mandy. And he out of me. I think of Dolores and what she brings out of me. She has certainly given me a whole new perspective on life, and on grief—even on death.

The way we sat in that restaurant last night, you would have needed a microscope to spot that we were two grieving women. Maybe, for those few hours, we weren't. Maybe that's what we bring out of each other.

My phone buzzes and whereas before I would have ignored it, I can't do that any longer because it might be a message from Dolores and I can't miss that.

It's from Jeremy asking what I'm doing tonight. I'm reluctant to make plans with him because, even though

Dolores and I are only going on a coffee date, I want to keep my options open. Although, in the back of my mind, the thought has nestled itself that I might also be afraid to sleep with her. Because this time, it would be different. Much more deliberate. When I rip her clothes off her—oh God, that red dress she wore so expertly last night—this time, my hand won't be steered by grief and a willingness to forget. On the contrary. I'll be wanting to make a memory so as never to forget the time we began dating officially.

I brush Jeremy off, saying that I need an early night because I'm starting work again tomorrow. Another reason not to spend the night with Dolores. Though, perhaps, I need her to wipe me out, to quiet the nerves that come with the requirements of the part of my job that's new.

I rifle through more of Ian's drawings and, sure enough, as though he's sending me some sign from the afterlife, there's one of Dolores. At least I think it's supposed to be her. I look for a date he might have scribbled on the back, but can't find any. When did he draw this? Maybe Dolores knows, or maybe she doesn't and seeing the drawing will only rack up more memories. I flick through some more, trying to forget about the portrait of Dolores.

Portraits weren't his strong suit, but inanimate objects tweaked with his own vision of a future he would never experience were. There's a drawing of a building with all sorts of curved cone-likes shapes on its roof. There's a triple-decker bridge. A bicycle with the same kind of wings as the car. I'll have to give Dolores some of these, she would like that.

Another message arrives on my phone. This time it *is* from Dolores.

*Want to come to mine?*

\* \* \*

While I couldn't resist meeting Dolores at her house, I go with a steely resolve to not let the possibilities of being alone together deter me from taking this slowly. I wonder why she changed our plans. We were meant to meet in a coffee shop downtown, as friends would, or two people on a second date. For me, there was also the addition of doing something in public, which makes it more proper, more like real dating.

When she opens the door, she smiles broadly, pulls me inside and gathers me in her arms. She only kisses me on the cheek.

"Where in Chicago can you get a better cappuccino?" she asks once we're in the kitchen, her voice coquettish and high.

"It's not really about the quality of the coffee, is it?"

Dolores looks at me with mock-amazement. "Is that you, Sophie? Or did someone else's soul slip into your body?"

I have to chuckle at her playfulness. Her mood seems light as air today. She's flirting, firing on all cylinders.

Once seated, with deliciously steaming cups of coffee in front of us, I say, "You know why I wanted to meet at a coffee shop."

"Hm." She fixes me with a stare. "Yes, I know it's not about the coffee." A sudden gloominess washes over her face.

"What's wrong?" I always feel so silly asking that question—after Ian.

"This is my house. I've lived here for a very, very long time. I have a lot of memories here, but… since you left… it's different. I can't find my groove in my own house anymore. It's not the same without you here. I guess I just wanted to see you sitting at my kitchen table again, drinking my coffee, even just see you walk through the front door, though it was strange to actually open the door for you."

"Is this where you ask me to move in?" I joke, hiding how her words really make me feel. Wanted. Desired beyond belief. Loved.

She shakes her head. "I know things started strangely between us, with everything in the wrong order, and you now want to undo this by dating 'properly'." She bends her fingers into quotation marks. "And I get it, I really do. I understand the thought process behind it. In my head, it makes sense... in my heart, not so much."

"What are you saying?" I hide most of my face behind my coffee cup.

"Nothing. I don't know." She sighs. "I'm saying that I've missed you and that I have no idea how to take things slowly with you because it doesn't make any sense after all we've been through and all we've done. It feels like taking a step back. And then, well, there's also something else." She taps her fingers—her nails still painted red—on the tabletop. "I'm afraid. When you left, it hurt me too. And despite working long hours, I had too much time to think about us and to wonder about the difference between what you mean to me and what I can mean to you."

"Oh, Dolores." I fight the urge to get up and throw my arms around her.

"You left so easily, like it was nothing. One minute we were arguing in the hallway, the next you'd packed your belongings and you were out of here." She holds up her hands. "I know *why* you left. I know that I pushed you, but the swiftness of it all hurt me. You may think I'm made of steel, that I'm so strong, but I'm not. I have feelings too."

"I know that." I do get up this time. "That's why I believed this had to be a slow process for us the second time around. So that we can gauge our feelings along the way and —"

Dolores pushes her chair back. "But that's just the thing, Sophie. I don't need to gauge my feelings for you anymore. I know what I feel. I know it when I look at you. I know it as I sit here. I knew it all along while you were at Jeremy's and I knew it even more after I sent you that email and you never replied." She stands. "Ours may be a love born from the most dire circumstances, and it may be frowned upon by many, and it may be doomed, who knows?

But that doesn't make it any less. I don't need to get to know you any more. I know you already. I know all I need to know. Except for one thing."

I'm the one who takes the first step toward her. I'm the one who wraps my fingers around her wrists and tugs her close. "I think you know that too."

"Maybe I do," she mutters.

When we kiss, all the words she just spoke mingle in my head, until they scream only one sentence, loud and clear: Dolores loves me.

"I'll date you all you want, Sophie," Dolores whispers in my ear in between breathless lip-locks. "Just as long as you know that I don't need to do so to know. I knew enough yesterday."

"So did I," I reply, before losing the power of speech again, and having the rest of my words swallowed by her eager mouth on mine.

When Dolores decides we're not taking things slowly, we don't.

# CHAPTER THIRTY-FIVE

●●●●●●●●●●●●●●●●●●●●●

The next Friday, when I arrive at Dolores' house—letting myself in with the key she gave me long ago—Dolores pounces on me as soon as I make my way into the hallway. She's wearing the same red dress she wore on our date last week, the same red lipstick, and a hell of a crooked grin on her face.

"What's with the welcoming committee?" I ask, as soon as my lips are no longer occupied with kissing hers.

"I'm glad it's the weekend, that's all." She keeps planting kisses on the side of my neck.

"What about the attire? Are we meant to go somewhere?" This is the first real semi-busy week I've had, what with starting work again, and I rack my brain for a social engagement I might have missed, which is silly, because Dolores and I don't have a social life together. Not yet. "Or did I get my dates mixed up?" I take a step back and give Dolores an appreciative once-over.

"I wouldn't dress like this for anyone else, Sophie." She has a sparkle in her eyes that's shinier than any I've seen before. "But I wanted to recreate some of the atmosphere of last week's date. I think we both agreed that was a *really* good date."

She barely gives me time to nod. She comes for me again, wrapping her arms around me, her mouth close to my ear. "A few weeks ago, I got you—well, us, I guess—a present, and let's just say it was on my mind all throughout that date."

"Oh really?"

"We never got a chance to… use it, and I thought tonight would be a good night for it." The smile that appears on her lips is wicked enough to inform me that she got me —or us—a sex toy. I'm not that naive.

A pulse starts underneath my skin. The past week, we've taken it sort of slow—somewhere in the middle of where we both wanted things to be. But if this week confirmed one thing, it's that what we feel for each other is strong enough to not let go of, to not make light of and write off as merely two people finding each other on the darkest side of grief. We've crossed over. Not just over the line of decency we demolished weeks ago when we first kissed, but from secret lovers to two women in a relationship.

A first step away from the women we were when we grew close. A first step to overcoming the despair Ian's accident plunged us into. A first step to, together, being more than two women in pain. A first step into a brand new life. A life without Ian. My boyfriend; her son. Together, we are more than the sum of our pain. There's endless chemistry and all this love and the roots of something more, but, for me, there's also a confirmation that, as of now, I *can* look to the future. When I do, I see the future I tried to describe to Jeremy that day, even though I'm well aware we don't live in an ideal world.

I might be foolish, we might both be foolish, but we haven't lost our minds.

"I guess I could use a little decompression after my first week back at work," I say.

"Let's go straight upstairs then." Dolores takes my hand, interweaves her fingers with mine, and we bolt up the stairs.

"Sit down. Make yourself comfortable on the bed. I'll be right back." Before she goes, Dolores curls her arms around my neck and kisses me, her tongue probing deep from the get-go. Then she heads into the bathroom.

I sit on the bed, my skin prickling with excitement, and wonder exactly how comfortable I should make myself. Should I start removing garments? I start with my shoes but leave it there. I want Dolores' hands on me, want her fingers to skim along my skin when she pulls my dress over my head.

I wait, my heart full of lust and my head filled with images of Dolores. Her red-lipped smile at the restaurant last week. The inviting slope of her cleavage. Her desire for me so on display. How wanted she made me feel just by being there. Seeing her again at Starbucks before that and the shock it delivered to my system. I've barely even thought about Albert the truck driver anymore. Maybe because it wasn't his fault. Or maybe because the effect Dolores has on me is too intoxicating, too all-consuming. I remember what I wrote in my last letter to Ian. *I should not be falling in love with your mother.* But who decides what should and shouldn't happen in my life? Isn't that up to me?

Then Dolores exits the bathroom—empty-handed. At first glimpse, everything looks exactly the same as when she entered it. Then she sets her hip a certain way, juts it forward a little, her hands on her sides, and I see something bulge underneath her dress.

Oh.

Eyes narrowed, she walks over to me, pulls me up by my hands, and presses herself against me. "What do you think, Sophie?" Her voice is a thin whisper in my ear.

I don't need to see to know exactly what she's hiding underneath that dress. I'm so aroused, and a little surprised, I can't make any words come out of my mouth.

Dolores kisses her way from my ear to my lips, then pushes herself back for a second to look at me. There's no more smile on her face. "Sophie?"

I don't say anything, just pull her close again, lose myself in the most intoxicating kiss. I can't wait for her to take off that dress. I can't wait to see it. I can't wait for her to slip it inside of me.

"Show me," I say, and sit back down.

"Take off your dress first." Dolores' voice is low and hoarse.

I quickly pull it over my head, throw it on the floor.

Then, Dolores, ever so slowly, starts pulling up her dress. The red fabric slides over her thigh. She fixes her gaze on me. Then she pulls the garment over her head in one go, revealing a pretty sizable dildo fastened in a pair of bright red boy shorts—almost the same color as the dress she just removed. The dildo is violet and has an immediate effect on my level of excitement.

As though in a trance, I slither off the bed, and kneel in front of Dolores. In front of her present for me—for us. What is this doing to her? We have so many more dates to go on to process all of this, but why should we even attempt to put this into words, when we can just show each other what this, all of this, is doing to us. I'll show her now.

I plant my lips on the toy. It smells rubbery, not-human, strange, but I'm overcome by an unstoppable urge to take it into my mouth. This is me reduced to my most base desires. This is me in front of Dolores, about to give her everything I have left in me, again. Or no, it's not that, I think when I open my lips over the head of the dildo. I'm not giving her anything. I'm restoring myself. I'm putting myself back together, tiny piece by tiny piece, with her, by acknowledging this lust, this fire between us, this inevitableness, this bond. And how I move my mouth along this dildo Dolores bought for us to play with, is all part of it. Everything is. From that night she asked me if I wanted to stay here, and us meeting in the darkness of the night in Ian's old bedroom, and me ending up in her bed, my mind on nothing like this at all. My soul so shattered all I could see and think was blackness. And how, night after night, we crept closer inch by inch until there was no space left between us.

This is us now. This is my desire unbuckled, my lust unleashed. Because I'm alive and I want to live. These are our truest moments. This is what I've missed the most. Dolores so close to me there's no room for my grief to spill over into self-pity. I love her. I love this toy she got for us. I love how it says that she, too, believed we weren't done yet.

My lips skate over the dildo and I take it deep into my mouth, as deep as I can, and while the tip goes as far as it can go, I do have a flimsy second during which I come to and wonder how I came to be kneeling in Dolores' bedroom with my lips clasped around a dildo.

Then Dolores' hands are in my hair and the moment of clarity is eclipsed by her touch and by the intensity of what I'm doing. This is just like that first kiss, I think, only more. A moment during which I let go of inhibitions completely and follow my gut. This time, I have no regrets.

I let the toy slip from my lips, and look at it. It's all slick and wet. How did Dolores know this would turn me on so much? It was probably a gamble. Or experience. I push myself up and sit on the bed, immediately scooting backwards. I'm still wearing my panties, but I want *her* to take them off.

Dolores hops onto the bed with me, the toy dangling deliciously between her legs. She comes to lie half on top of me and the dildo presses against my thigh. The saliva I covered it in leaves a wet patch on my skin while Dolores kisses me and I kiss her back with more zest than I knew I had in me.

Her hands roam across my skin, fumble with my bra cups, set my breasts free. Her fingers pinch my nipples, her teeth bite my skin.

"God, I've missed you," she whispers in my ear when her mouth hovers there. "I've missed you so much."

I'm the least me and the most me I can possibly be. With Dolores, I come home every time, whether she prepares me a meal, puts a gentle hand on my shoulder, or is about to fuck me with a strap-on dildo. With her, everything always feels way beyond any sensation of feeling good I should be allowed to have only four months after losing my life partner. She has turned everything upside down for me.

She kisses her way down my torso, maneuvers my panties off—and I help her greedily. Then, she sits between my legs, silicone cock at the ready. It's the most strange and exhilarating sight I've ever seen. It's bewildering and arousing and sets my skin on fire.

Dolores brings her hands behind her back and takes off her bra, only adding to the sensuality of the picture in front of me. My entire body is flooded with yearning. My clit throbs out of control. My skin sizzles with anticipation. My mind is a blank slate because it has already fully surrendered to this moment. To her.

I spread wide for her, making it clear, I hope, that I'm ready for this.

Dolores shuffles closer, the movement of her knees making the mattress quake a little. She's so close, I can feel the tip of the dildo against my inner thigh. Dolores scans my face.

"Please," I murmur, to spur her on. My voice is just a flimsy whimper. Just an instrument for begging.

She inches nearer and I feel the insistence of the toy now, its rigidness. She palms it and, ever so gently, slides the tip over my wet, wet pussy lips. It's as though I can feel myself open up for her. The dildo slips and slides with a bit more intent now and seeing it between Dolores' fingers like that is more of a turn-on than anything else. She's a power lesbian all right, the very definition of one. Outside the bedroom and in. In my head, I compose a line for the article about her I will never write. *The way she holds a dildo between her fingers, so delicately but masterfully, is enough to make any woman want her. Thus is the power of the power lesbian.* It's silly, and perhaps the beginning of an inside joke between us. Something to remember how this all began.

Then Dolores' fingers are between my legs, gliding along my pussy where the dildo did before. If she's gauging my wetness, my receptiveness for her and her toy, it can't be misinterpreted. My clit buzzes as though wanting to scream, *Yes, I'm ready.*

"Fuck me, please." There's my begging whimper of a voice again. I seem to have lost control over it. Nothing my body is doing right now is conventional, or expected of a mourning widow. Dolores and I, we've violently cast off any expectations the world may have of us and we've created our own. No one else will dictate the amount of grief we're supposed to feel, the amount of time for us to hide away and suffer. What we do here in this bed in her room is our decision, our way of giving the finger to death and its grim, ever-lasting consequences.

Dolores rubs her wet fingers over the toy, making it all slick again. I crane my neck to get a better view—this is a show I don't want to miss—and the violet of the dildo glistens in the low light of the room. Dolores' eyes shine. And my heart is about to burst out of my chest.

Then, at last, she brings the toy to my entrance and, slowly, inch by inch, pushes inside. This is an entirely different sensation than having her fingers inside me. With this toy, which isn't even part of her body but might as well be, it's as though she takes possession of me—as if she didn't have me already. It says she loves me in all the ways words fail. It cuts off my breath when she pushes deep, when she spreads me wide, when she claims me.

She folds her body over mine, thrusting gently, holding herself up on her arms, gazing into my eyes. I fear I might faint because of too much sensation. Too much of everything. Too much of her, of us. We are so close, everything else seems far away. The things we did when perhaps we shouldn't have and the ones we didn't when we really wanted to.

Dolores looks at me when she fucks me and I try to

keep my eyes open, try to drink in every little grimace of her face, her beautiful, beautiful face with that radiant smile, that is serious now, because this is serious business. This is *our* toy, *our* moment of reunion. Perhaps it's the beginning of the rest of our lives or whatever this may become. Neither one of us has that crystal ball, and the odds might be against us, but here and now, everything, every last atom in the atmosphere, is in favor of us.

Dolores ups the pace and I start meeting her thrusts with my pelvis, start losing my mind a little, because this might be the most surreal moment of my life. Dolores fucking me like this is not something I could ever have imagined, just like so many other things that have happened between us. But this—this pleasure, this surrender, this yielding of my body to hers—is the pinnacle. It's everything. It's much more than I could have hoped for in this wretched post-Ian life in which all I have is his ghost and memories that hurt because they can't be relived properly and a bunch of letters I've written him.

What is happening between us now is purely carnal, it's two bodies going at it, expressing through base instincts what is in our hearts. It's not just longing and desire, but also the expulsion of pain, of nights spent alone and awake, of thoughts of a future so bleak and teary it made us cry just conjuring it up. Perhaps that's why Dolores' strokes inside of me are so fierce. But it's nothing I can't take. I match her every thrust, accompanied by a guttural groan, and each one makes my flesh sing more, makes my pleasure more pure, takes me to this place I could never reach alone.

Dolores blinks a couple of times, as though she stepped out of her body and is only now coming to. She stops thrusting and says, "Come sit on top of me."

I nod and she slides out of me. As quick as I can, I straddle her, surely dripping wetness everywhere, that's how aroused I am, and lower myself onto the toy she holds up with both hands. Once it is inside me, I find a good angle, and while I do, Dolores expertly unclasps the bra I'm still wearing and tosses it somewhere into the room.

She cups my breasts with her hands, slips my nipples between her fingers, and we find a new rhythm.

"You're so beautiful," she whispers, but I understand. Each of my senses is heightened. I hear the rustle of the sheets beneath our writhing bodies. I smell the perfume of my sex all around us. I see every tiny expression her face makes. I see how the corners of her mouth curl up every time I push myself down and she meets me halfway. I see the glimmer in her eyes that I choose to interpret as love. I see—

I stop seeing things when Dolores brings a hand between my legs and touches a finger lightly to my clit. Oh fuck, I'm about to lose it entirely.

She circles my clit gently, to the rhythm of my slowed thrusts. When I go faster, she goes faster. We understand each other in this also. I feel part of her, I feel as though our bodies have melded together and when I open my eyes, I see her pleasure, and it escalates mine.

The dildo inside of me, her finger on my clit, her hand on my breast, Dolores below me. It's enough. More than enough. I fall over the edge of where lust transforms into pleasure. I fall and I fall and I scream and I howl. I let go completely. In this moment, I let go of the pain that brought us together. The pain that we made into this.

"Oh fuck," I stammer when I collapse into her receiving arms. My cheeks are wet from too much emotion, too much rapture. I try to hold the words back, but I'm too spent, so I say, "I love you." It's nothing but the absolute truth, after all. Nothing Dolores didn't already know. But to say it like this, in this moment, makes it sound different. Like the romantic kind of love I believed to be impossible between us. So it startles me a little too.

"I love you too." Dolores wraps her arms around me so tightly I can barely breathe. My face is squashed against her chest, surely leaving a tiny puddle of tears between her breasts. "Oh, I do." Only when her embrace loses a little of its power, do I push myself away from her, take a deep breath and look at her. There are beads of sweat on her forehead, and a tiny smile on her lips, but no sign of tears in her eyes.

I look at her and am even more overwhelmed with love. I wipe the wetness from my cheeks with the back of my hand and lie next to her, an arm slung over her chest. "When did you buy this... present?" I press a kiss to her cheek.

She turns on her side and we face each other. "A few weeks ago. I guess I was waiting for the right time to introduce it."

I glance at the toy still stickily pointing upwards between her legs. I wouldn't mind trying it on myself some time, but not tonight. Tonight, I'm spent, but not too spent to push my own fingers inside of Dolores. To give her what she gave me.

"Why don't you take it off?"

Dolores nods, does a quick raising of the eyebrows, then works the shorts and dildo off while the tip of her tongue sticks out of her mouth.

"Let me see if this has in any way aroused you. It would surprise me if it had, but let me have a feel, anyway." I give her the biggest smirk I have in me.

She spreads her legs, eagerness lighting up her face. "Let me know," she says, takes my hand, and brings it to her wetness.

* * *

When I wake up, Dolores is still fast asleep. I look at her in the morning light, then stretch my arms over my head, luxuriating in the fact that I'm back in her bed, still glowing from last night's activities. I don't look at the alarm clock. I don't care what time it is. It's Saturday and I have nowhere to be.

I do know, however, that it's important for me not to stay over again tonight. I'll need to go back to my place—I can almost call it that without flinching now. Need to reclaim my independence a little bit more, the way I've been doing since I left Jeremy's.

Next to me, Dolores starts stirring and I watch her as she wakes up. Her eyelids flutter a few times, then she opens them. When she sees me looking at her, she smiles, and I can feel her smile radiate deep inside of me.

"Morning," she says, and reaches for me, pulling me close. "What a night, huh?" she whispers into my ear. "Maybe we should do that again some time."

"Maybe." Dolores' eagerness for me after we started seeing each other again keeps astounding me.

"What are you doing tonight?" she asks.

"Maybe I'll cook you dinner at my place."

"Will you now?"

"We could also do take-out, I guess."

"How about I cook *you* dinner at *your* place?" No hesitation before the *your*.

"Sounds very tempting." Beneath the sheets, I press a hand against her warm belly.

"Do we need to talk about this? Process our situation, perhaps? Set some ground rules?"

Dolores gives a light chuckle. "I'm not so big on rules. Besides, rules won't save us, Sophie. We're already so depraved. Look at us in bed together."

"Utterly contemptuous." I try to mimic an upper-crust British accent and it makes me think of Ian.

"Here's my suggestion." Dolores sounds a bit more serious. "Let's just do this the only way we can: take it one day at a time. See where that leads us. I want you in my life. In this very capacity." Her hand flattens mine against her belly. "No other will do, for now. Which doesn't mean that I don't want you to be totally honest with me because honesty is all we have. It's the very foundation of what we're doing.

If, one day, you don't want this anymore, you need to tell me. I need to know that's what you will do. Otherwise, this can't work."

"I want you in my life too and all the same goes for you."

"Okay." Her fingers intertwine with mine.

"Good."

"We should probably give that toy a good scrub." Dolores inches her face closer and kisses me on the nose. The entire room smells of sex, of exquisite times had. If love had a smell, it would smell of that too.

"Yes, because it's my turn today." A tingle takes root in my stomach.

"I'm not sure that's a good idea." Dolores frowns.

"Why not?"

"I think I hurt my back last night. Serves me right for doing something I haven't done in a decade at my age." The grin she paints on gives away that she's just joking.

"I thought dating someone younger was supposed to keep you young and spritely?"

"I guess it hasn't rubbed off on me yet." She inches her entire body closer. "You're going to have to rub me a bit more."

"I guess I have no choice but to respect my elders."

We both break out into a chuckle. The room is fully illuminated by a bright mid-morning sun. Dolores' eyes sparkle in the light, mirroring how I feel inside.

# CHAPTER THIRTY-SIX

Ian,

I know I haven't written for a while. I've been busy and... I've also been seeing your mother. I guess I should call it dating, but it doesn't feel like dating. Not like the dating you and I did. I know Dolores so well already because of what we've been through.

Let me give you a quick update of everything that has happened. I'm back at work. I write part-time for The Post's weekend magazine and the rest of my time I devote to investigative journalism. It's good to have that old part of myself back, but to also have found something new. I do write the more fluffier pieces now, but I try to keep it interesting for myself. I'm trying to convince Dolores to let me write a piece on her, but she won't allow it. Even when I threaten to find other power lesbians to interview.

I've decided to sell our apartment. I've lived there for two months now and while I think it was important to return, to face some facts, I don't think my future is there. It's too much you. It was your apartment before I moved in and before you left it to me. Everything reminds me of you in a way that is hard to deal with sometimes. As if I'm not reminded of you every minute of every day already. I'll put it on the market and then rent somewhere. I need a place where I can start anew, where I can put your things in a spot that I choose for them as opposed to them having been in that spot forever, or at least since you were still alive.

In case you're wondering, I still miss you every day. Every hour of every day even though it's not like we were together every hour when you were still alive. It's because of the sudden brutality with which you *were taken from me, from all of us. The brusque cruelty of it all.*

*Dolores and I talk about you more. In the beginning, after we started 'dating' it was often awkward, as if we no longer knew how to broach the subject of you, even though we'd talked so much about you before. After meeting with that truck driver and the things that happened afterwards, it felt as though some sort of barrier had been put up. Like if we talked about you too much it would ruin the magic of what we had between us. We talk about that too now, because once we started talking about you again, we could talk about anything.*

*I guess what I'm really trying to say is that Dolores and I are in a relationship now.*

*I know how it sounds, especially to you. I could give you a long speech about how Dolores saved me from the worst of it, how she made me see some light in a darkness I could not ever imagine receding, and perhaps there might be some truth to those things, but, you know what? The very simple fact is that I fell in love with her. We fell in love with each other.*

*It was very difficult to tell Alex—who is about to pop, by the way. She and Bart are having a little girl. She couldn't believe it at first when I told her. She thought I had lost my mind and was ranting and raving or that I was under the influence of a very powerful drug. In the end, she hugged me and told me to do whatever made me happy. As simple as that.*

*Of course, at work, where I have actual colleagues now with whom I go to bars for after-work drinks and such, nobody asks me about my private life too much. They all know what happened to you, which, ironically, saves me from having to answer difficult questions about how I've spent my weekend.*

*I guess what I'm also trying to say is that things are as good as can be expected with me, maybe even better. It's only been six months and perhaps I should still be plunged deeply into mourning. Had it not been for Dolores, I probably still would be, but I know for a fact how much you would hate that. You, the person who hated self-pity more than anything. The guy who gave me a stern talking to every time I only lightly veered in that direction.*

*Oh, and in case you're wondering: no, I haven't told my parents yet. Granted, my mother and I are not close, but that doesn't mean I want to give her a heart attack. And it would only give her one more subject to yammer on about. You know, about how it affects her personally and all of that.*

*You must realize, Ian, that what drew me to Dolores in the beginning was her strength. The exact same thing that drew me to you.*

*She makes me happy at a time where I'm not meant to experience happiness. Is it always easy? Hell no. Not for either of us. But you know what? We mostly don't care. Because we know what it's like to have loved and lost, and in the face of that, what's a sneer from someone who doesn't care enough about us to even try to understand?*

*That's what it boils down to. If there has to be a lesson to all of this, that's what your death has taught me.*

*I love you, always.*

*Sophie*

# CHAPTER THIRTY-SEVEN

●●●●●●●●●●●●●●●●●●●

"If you don't want to be here," Jeremy says, "please, feel free to leave." He angles his head and gives me one of his looks.

"I'm sorry." I can't stop glancing at my watch. Usually, when I spend time with Jeremy, it flies by. For once, he called *me* in distress, wanting to talk to me about an issue he's having. "It's so nerve-wracking." Dolores is having dinner with her friend June. The plan was to tell June all about us.

"June is a good old sport," Jeremy says. "She may grumble a little, but she'll get over it." He holds up his empty glass, indicating I should pour more wine. "Now back to me." He pouts his lips. "Why is it so difficult for Vasily and me? Look at you and Dolores. You lesbians make it look so easy."

I pour Jeremy a generous helping, then shake my head. "Please. You just enjoy the drama that comes with making it so hard on yourself."

"But I really like him, Soph. I don't think he even realizes how much."

"Then tell him. Make it so clear to him, he doesn't have a choice but to respond." The conversation Jeremy and I have been having for the past hour keeps going around in circles. He's acting like a school boy with his very first crush.

Jeremy sighs. "You know it doesn't work that way."

"Then let me tell you this, my friend." In the past, I've always patiently listened to Jeremy's tales of men he *really, really* likes, and all the reasons he has for not disclosing that information to the object of his affection. Today, my patience seems to be running very thin. "If it's meant to be, it will happen. Just stop making it all so complicated. You like him. From what you've told me, I gather he likes you. What's the problem?"

"You know my relationship track record." Jeremy shakes his head. "It's not that good."

"It doesn't matter. Besides, I think it's about time you settled down. You'll be forty-five in two short years. Don't you get tired of all that drama all the time?"

"That's not the point, Soph." Jeremy doesn't take offense at me mentioning his age. He must really have it bad.

"It *is* the point." I find his glance. "Look at me and Dolores. We are the most unlikely couple. If that is possible, why wouldn't it be possible for you and Vasily, who have nothing standing in your way, apart from your egos and a, frankly, silly fear of commitment. This is the part you're meant to enjoy the hell out of. The butterflies. The tingle in your belly when you're about to call him. The way your heart leaps when he turns the corner. Don't overthink it. Just go for it. Because life is short and, hm, who was it that told me you should get your pleasure where you can? It was this friend of mine…"

Jeremy folds his features into a smile. Then he starts toying with his phone.

"Call him. Now," I say. "What have you got to lose?"

As if by magic, a phone starts ringing. It's not Jeremy's. It's mine.

"It's Dolores." I know it's silly, but my heart starts hammering in my chest. It's a big step for her to tell June.

"Sophie, are you at home?" There's a funny crack in her voice.

"I'm at Vesuvio's with Jeremy."

"Stay there. I'm coming over."

Before I have a chance to ask how things went, she hangs up, leaving me with a slew of questions.

"And?" Jeremy arches up his eyebrows.

"I don't know. She's coming here."

"Ooh," he coos. "Exciting. Do you want me to go?"

"No, but I do want you to at least message Vasily. Don't play so hard to get. It will get you nowhere." Because it's all so brittle, so easy to splinter and just slip through your fingers when you're not paying attention, I want to say. "Don't squander this chance you have."

* * *

By the time Dolores arrives, Jeremy is frantically texting back and forth with Vasily, a constant smile playing on his lips.

"Give me some of that, honey," Dolores says, pointing at the wine, even before she kisses me hello.

"That bad?" I ask.

She slips onto one of the high stools, gives Jeremy a quick nod, and says, "Worse."

"What did she say?" Jeremy's attention is no longer focused on his flirty text message conversation.

"At first, she thought I was joking. That it couldn't possibly be true. When I assured her we were really together, she accused me of taking advantage of you. Of abusing your grief in the worst possible manner."

"Christ." I take a big gulp of wine.

"That's harsh," Jeremy says.

"I suppose I should have expected to lose some acquaintances over this, but not a friend like June. Someone who knows me so well. At least enough to know I would never do that." Dolores' voice fractures. She looks at me. "You don't feel taken advantage of, do you?"

"If anything, I took advantage of you," I say.

"It's all a matter of perception," Jeremy chimes in. "You're the older lesbian, Dolores. Sophie is the younger, vulnerable girl who got her heart broken when her boyfriend died. It's an image that's not easy to get past."

"But she's my friend." Dolores looks lost. She usually looks so good, so well-put-together, when she goes out to meet a friend.

"Maybe she just needs some time," I offer. "This has

been our reality for a while, but I guess when you've just been told, it's quite shocking."

"I believe she used the word *scandalous*." Dolores drinks more wine. She shrugs. "Who needs a friend like that?"

"I'm sorry." Under the table, I put a hand on her knee.

"Shocking or not, I believe I'm entitled to some open-mindedness from a woman I've known forever, especially after everything that has happened."

I glance at Dolores who, even with the lines around her mouth set in a stern frown and the sparkle in her eyes dimmed, still is the most beautiful woman I've ever seen. The world is far from ideal and the relationship we've decided to have, that has chosen us, and helped us overcome the sharpest pains of grief, won't be accepted by everyone.

* * *

Later, at Dolores' house, when we're lying in the bed where it all started, I ask, "Will you be able to sleep?"

Dolores pats my head that's tucked cozily into the crook of her shoulder. "I will. And you know why? Because I know what we have between us and I know it's the opposite of all the things June thinks it is."

"We've weathered worse storms," I murmur.

"Much worse." Dolores strokes my cheeks. "I did try to put myself in her position. I imagined June telling me that she had started a relationship with her son-in-law after her daughter had died. I know what it sounds like, what it looks like. I can even understand, but what we have is not a gimmick, it's not a joke, it's not the one-line plot of a trashy porn movie. Perhaps I failed to make her see that, to make her fully understand what you mean to me. Like Jeremy said, it's all a matter of perspective, but it's also so much more than that. People can be so quick to judge, even when they know your story. June knows our story. To be reduced by her to… a scandal. That hurts."

"Well, our love *is* scandalous, of course."

"It's scandalous and delicious and soothing and healing

216

and glorious and beautiful and important," she says. "It's all these things."

"But to some you will also be the cougar lesbian who seduced me when I was at my most frail."

"While it was you who kissed me." Dolores chuckles. "Twice."

I push myself up a little so I can see her face. "What did you think when I kissed you? *Finally?*"

Dolores shakes her. "All I thought about was how much I had grown to love you and depend on you. That's all." The sincerity in her tone touches me. "Because isn't that what this is, after all has been said and done? It's love. It's as simple as that."

While I kiss Dolores on the lips, I consider that maybe I should have a little chat with June.

# CHAPTER THIRTY-EIGHT

●●●●●●●●●●●●●●●●●●●●●

I ring June's bell three days after her conversation with Dolores, figuring that should be enough time for her to have absorbed most of the shock.

"Sophie? What are you doing here?" I fully understand her surprise at me turning up at her doorstep. I've been to her house a couple of times before with Ian, of whom June was very fond, but we certainly never turned up out of the blue like this.

"Good evening, June. I think you and I should share a bottle of good wine tonight. I hope you're free?" I didn't tell Dolores I was coming here. I'm sure she wouldn't want me to do her bidding for her, but she can tell me all day and night that June's judgment about our relationship doesn't affect her, I can clearly tell it does.

"Er, well, yes. Come in." She opens the door to me.

Once seated, each with a glass of wine in front of us, I launch into the speech I have rehearsed all day.

"I know you loved Ian, June. You knew him his entire life, watched him grow up. Dolores is your friend, which made Ian your friend. But no one loves him more than Dolores and I do. And what we have between us doesn't taint his memory, not for us. Ian's death brought us together, but—"

June doesn't let me finish. She holds up her hand. "You don't have to spell it out for me, Sophie. I don't need a lecture."

*But I need to say this,* I think. *Not just for you, but for myself as well.* "Okay." I shouldn't forget that my only objective for this visit is convincing June that Dolores didn't take advantage of my grief.

"It's not as if I didn't know something was going on with Dolores. When we talked, it always felt as if she was leaving something out. I thought it was the loss of Ian making her act a little funny. It made sense that way. But when she told me about you and her. Not in a million years had I expected that."

"I know it's a little shocking."

"A little?" She expels a quick breath. "You think you know someone…"

"That kind of works both ways, don't you think?"

June narrows her eyes. "I'm not finished, Sophie. Let me speak."

I almost say "Yes, Ma'am," but manage to swallow it with a big gulp of wine.

"Of course it's shocking and upsetting. To think it had been going on for months. All behind my back, of course. For which I might be grateful if it wasn't such a big thing for Dolores." June takes a deep breath, drinks from her wine.

By now, I've learned not to interrupt.

"Do you love her… the same way she loves you?" she asks in a stern tone. I wonder where the big spotlight is that cops use in movies to get their suspects to confess.

"I do. I love her. I was the one who started it all. Dolores is just… so many things. You know her, so you know." There goes my eloquence. Fat load of good rehearsing that speech did me.

"Then that's all I need to know." Her voice softens. "You turning up here says enough anyway."

I sigh with relief.

"Not everyone is going to be as easygoing about this as me," she says.

"Easygoing?" I give her a big frown. "That's what you call easygoing?"

"I just want Dolores to be happy. That's really, truly, all

I want for her. After losing Angela and then Ian, she deserves a little bit of happiness. A little bit of comfort. Something that makes her feel good. Not everyone will feel the same. Being with you might make her feel good, but having to battle other people's opinions about it won't feel so good."

"I'm well aware."

"Hold on for a minute, will you." June rises and disappears from the living room.

When she comes back, she's holding a cardboard model of a very futuristic-looking house. Seeing it is like a dart puncturing the spot in my belly where most of the pain first settled. She doesn't need to tell me it's Ian's. I know.

"He made this when he was only a boy. Twelve or thirteen, I think," June says. "He already knew he wanted to be an architect. He made that dream come true, and not many of us do, Sophie. Most of our childhood dreams don't come true." She holds it out to me. "It's yours now."

I feel tears pressing up. It's June's way of saying she's willing to accept my relationship with Ian's mother.

* * *

That night, in bed—I couldn't bear to stick to my own silly rule of no sleep-overs two nights in a row after my visit to June—we lie in silence for a while. My head rests on Dolores' chest and I can hear the sound of her breath. Her hand strokes all the way from the nape of my neck to the small of my back, up and down and up and down. It reminds me of how I used to lie in bed like this with Ian. Almost exactly the same way as I'm lying here with his mother, except that Ian's arms were longer and when he caressed me, his hand went all the way to my thighs.

Some things are the same, but most of them are very different. Because I'm different. I'm no longer a girl who will be caressed by Ian's long fingers, who will press her cheek against the dark, curly hair on his chest. I'm the girl who will always remember him and love him. And I'm the girl who won't do it alone.

I think of the model June gave me. Dolores broke down a little when I showed it to her. I told her it belonged in her house, not in my flat. He made it here. In his room, where we put it, back in its rightful place. In the room of a boy who dreamed of becoming an architect, and who became exactly that. *What else did he dream of?* I wonder, as I listen to Dolores' breathing, to the rustle of the sheet below her elbow as she keeps stroking my back. The usual things, I guess. Ordinary dreams of an extraordinary man. A man who lives on in the love Dolores and I share. Because no matter the dreams he had left, they'll never come true now. But, as my cheek sinks deeper against Dolores' flesh, I dare to guess that, in that brief moment between his losing his balance and his head hitting the sidewalk, he would have dreamed that I'd find some sort of peace after his death. All I want is for him to know, somehow, somewhere, that with Dolores, I have.

# EPILOGUE

● ● ● ● ● ● ● ● ● ● ● ● ● ● ● ● ● ● ● ●

At the party Dolores and I are throwing to commemorate what would have been Ian's thirty-seventh birthday, she's the one who gives a speech. Not everyone who felt compelled to come to his previous birthday is here, but it's close enough. Alex and Bart have brought their little girl, who is sleeping in a cot in my office upstairs. Dolores' colleagues from the gallery are there. Jeremy and his on-and-off boyfriend Vasily. All of mine and Ian's friends. June and a bunch of Dolores' arty friends. I invited my parents and for the longest time my mother insisted she and my dad wouldn't miss it, but she bailed at the last minute, which is not un-typical, I guess.

Booze has been flowing copiously for an hour or so and I, for one, am quite tipsy. I bought a new dress. I can keep my shoulders upright without having to make too much of an effort and the chit chat flows from my lips much better than last year, when I hardly said a word to anyone. When Dolores and I were still so broken, we ended up fumbling in the pantry, hiding away, trying to salvage something that couldn't possibly be salvaged.

Today, we're no longer hiding.

"Thank you all for coming and raising a glass in Ian's memory." There's a little crack in her voice, but these days, when her voice tends to break, it's not with the wretched grief that it used to show. Ian's death destroyed us, but we have started to rebuild. "I'm rather fond of the idea of making this a yearly tradition. Last year, when Sophie and I decided to have this party"—I'm standing right in front of Dolores and she fixes her gaze on me—"it was really because we had no clue what else to do with this day. With what it reminded us of. However, a year has gone by, and while all wounds have decidedly not yet healed, things are different now, just like they'll be different again one year from now."

Dolores blinks once and looks into the crowd again, but I can't keep my eyes off her.

"So you are a lesbian now?" Jeremy asked a couple of weeks ago, after I broke my lease and moved in with Dolores officially.

"Does the word bisexual mean anything to you?" I replied.

"Of course it does, Soph. My own boyfriend identifies as such."

"Then why are you being so obnoxious?"

"It's just my personality, darling. You know I can't help myself." He pecked me on the cheek and poured me some more brandy.

Most people we've told have come around in the end, even my parents. I blurted it out during a particularly taxing phone conversation with my mother one day.

"Dolores, Dolores, it's always Dolores with you," my mother said, being more right than she could probably imagine. She said it in her whiny, woe-is-me voice, the one I can stand the least, and I just told her.

"We're seeing each other," I said. "Romantically." That shut her up for a good long minute. To my surprise, she didn't hang up the phone there and then. I was glad for the little opening she left, for the words she spoke next, for not making it all about her for once.

"Does she make you happy?" she asked, and with it, erased a great deal of fear I'd had about having to tell her. Mere minutes later the conversation took a different turn, and she broke out in a tiny yelp of disbelief, but I was grateful for those few seconds of initial acceptance, even though it didn't last. What it told me was that there was a possibility this could be talked about at some point, Winters-family-style talk, but talk nonetheless.

It would have been better if she'd come today, but I understand. Different things are hard for different people.

I stop thinking about my own mother and look at Ian's mother instead. Since I told her that red is really her color she's bought a few new red dresses. "Just to please my lady," she said, and darted around the living room with one of them clasped against her body. She's wearing a red dress today and red lipstick and she looks gorgeous and in control and important—at least to me.

Dolores is the most important person in my life. She has been since Ian died. And we're still standing. We're still together. In an ideal world, we would have celebrated our first anniversary together already, but the world is far from ideal and we were both reluctant to start counting from the day we first got together. Instead, we've decided to use the day of meeting Albert the truck driver as the official beginning of our affair. The day of our first official date.

I tune back into Dolores' speech. I should be listening more attentively but I'm mesmerized by the red of her lips, by the shape of them, by the way she angles her head before she says something jokey.

"On behalf of Sophie and myself, I'd like to thank you once again for being here. Do stick around until the booze runs out." Dolores ends her speech with a big smile and by lifting her glass in the air.

"To Ian," everyone says, just like they did last year.

This time, I raise my glass with them. I put my hand up and keep my glance on Dolores. "To Ian," I say.

I still see him sometimes. Usually when I've drunk too much. I still go to Cooley's. I prefer it to going to his grave. I sit there and drink too much beer and, in my head, I talk to him. I tell him things. Ordinary things about my day at work or something funny that Dolores said. I no longer write him letters. I stopped doing that when I started on my first piece of serious investigative journalism again. A long article about illegal toxic waste dumping. Maybe someday I should write one about the consequences of not wearing a helmet when cycling. Someday, when I feel capable.

Dolores walks over to me, puts her hands on my shoulders and, in front of everyone, kisses me fully on the mouth.

"Come with me for a minute," she whispers in my ear after the kiss. "I need to show you something in the kitchen."

My brain is too fuzzy to realize what she's getting at, but as soon as we reach the kitchen, she closes the door behind us and drags me into the pantry. This time, we don't cry or break down or need each other in that raw, complicated way. This time, a year after the last time we were in there together, we exchange a kiss and a quick giggle and are out of there before it can raise any questions from our guests.

I walk back in the living room and look for Jeremy, but all his attention is focused on Vasily, who is such a nice guy. "Way too good for you," I keep telling Jeremy, in jest.

Upstairs, baby Juno starts crying and, as new parents tend to do, Alex stirs immediately and rushes upstairs.

Dolores grabs my hand and people cluster around us and we talk to them, hands clasped together.

The two of us standing in her living room like that, surrounded by friends and acquaintances, sums up this whole journey so perfectly.

Together, we made it through.

# ACKNOWLEDGEMENTS

Endless gratitude to my wife, the far superior part of our high-functioning co-dependent unit. When I started this story, and believed I was taking my cougar love one step too far (and the words came slower than I was comfortable with), she paid me a slew of very un-British compliments that got me past the doubts and fears that came with writing this book.

I respect no editor more than my trusted friend Cheyenne Blue, who never minces her words (she's the only one allowed to call me 'pompous') and always makes my books better.

Special mention to my beta reader Carrie (with whom I share a love for distinguished older women) who is so relentlessly nice, positive, and encouraging. I couldn't ask for a better first reader.

As always, my Launch Team are not only there for me when a book releases, but I get to avail of their support and smart wits whenever I need to. I'm well aware this is a great luxury.

Last but by no means least: Thank You, Dear Reader! Every single one of you has made a difference in my life. We are on this crazy lesfic journey together and, thanks to you, it's true what they say: There really is no better time to be a writer than right now.

Thank you all.

# ABOUT THE AUTHOR

Harper Bliss is the author of the novels *No Strings Attached,*
*The Road to You, Seasons of Love* and *At the Water's Edge,* the
*High Rise* series, the *French Kissing* serial and several other
lesbian erotica and romance titles. She is the co-founder of
Ladylit Publishing, an independent press focusing on lesbian
fiction. Harper lives on an outlying island in Hong Kong
with her wife and, regrettably, zero pets.

Harper loves hearing from readers and if you'd like to drop
her a note you can do so via harperbliss@gmail.com

Website: www.harperbliss.com
Facebook: facebook.com/HarperBliss
YouTube: youtube.com/c/HarperBliss